Christmas
AT TWIN FALLS

D0169481

Sugar and Spice Press
North Carolina, USA
www.sugarnspicepress.com

Nobody's Lover

TRESSIE LOCKWOOD

Chapter One

Cody stood up and pulled his jeans on. He left the button undone and the zipper down while he worked his boots on his feet. A moan sounded behind him, and he gritted his teeth. He'd hoped she wouldn't wake up before he got out of there.

She stretched with her arms over her head and allowed the sheet to slide down so her breasts were uncovered, but she no longer interested him. Even the kittenish purr did nothing. "Where are you going so early? I thought we would have breakfast together."

He frowned but didn't look at her. His boot finally on, he stood again and tugged his shirt over his head. Where did he leave his jacket—in the car or somewhere in her living room? "I have a ranch that won't run itself and cattle to feed."

"You've got hands to do that."

"Look, I had a good time last night, but that's all it was. I made that clear." He walked to the door, and when he stuck his hand out to grab the knob, a high heel hit the wall, just missing his head.

Nobody's Lover

"You're an asshole, Cody Everett. Get out! I don't ever want to see you again."

He stuffed his hat on his head and tapped it. Then walked out without another word. He resented her behaving like he owed her something. Sherrie was in that bar last night looking to find a man for her bed. They both knew that, and he'd been looking for the same thing—sex. A relationship wasn't on the menu, not now at least. This time of year, close to Christmas, all of his effort went into fighting depression. She didn't need to know that. No one did, not even his brother. Then again, Beau had his own issues around this time. Neither one of them had celebrated the holiday since their parents were killed. What would be the point?

He jumped into his truck and pulled out of the lot. As he drove along the highway, dawn just touched the horizon. He made out the shape of Cloud Peak Mountain, beyond his and his brother's ranch. He loved that scene, which meant home and safety. He couldn't believe he'd walked away from it for three years, leaving everything in Beau's hands. He was back now though—to stay.

Cody hit the button to lower his window a bit and breathed in the crisp Wyoming air. While it didn't exactly raise his spirits, it did clear his mind a bit from the night spent slugging back beers at the bar and chatting up women. He needed to focus on getting the barns cleaned out, feeding the cattle, and placing orders for more supplies.

TRESSIE LOCKWOOD

When the sign arching over Twin Falls Ranch came into view, he also spotted Henry, driving the tractor with the shovel fitted on the front. The snow hadn't been that bad, but he and Beau insisted all roads leading into and around their ranch be clear. He admitted they were anal about it, but who could blame them when their parents had been killed on an icy road.

Bringing the memory to mind constricted his breathing even after all this time, and he gripped the steering wheel tighter. He nodded at Henry as he drove by and caught the sound of Macaulay barking somewhere on the property. He pulled in front of his house and stepped out of the truck. A sharp, loud whistle brought his dog bounding to his side. Cody stooped to scratch behind Macaulay's ears.

"Hey, boy, whatcha doing? You keeping them in line? Not yet?" He chuckled. "I know, I know. I have to do my part, huh? Sorry for making you wait."

He knew he'd be sweaty and need another shower after work, but he took one anyway and changed his clothes. After supervising his hands to be sure the stalls in the buildings where he housed the cattle in winter were mucked out, he helped mix the feed. When that was done, he brought in bales of hay to dump in the troughs at the ends of the pens to round out his animals' diet.

Cody straightened from the last feeding and swiped an arm over his head. He always marveled at how he could sweat so much when the temperature in winter dropped so low.

"Hey, Cody."

Cody swiveled around at Henry's voice. "Hey, Henry. Things going okay?"

Henry nodded. "Nope. Was something like seventeen below this morning when I woke up. The missus going at me like it was something I ordered to piss her off."

Cody chuckled. "Yeah, well maybe she'll cheer up by lunchtime."

His ranch hand shook his head. "Wait until you find the right woman and settle down. Then you'll have more compassion for us guys who already fell into the trap."

"I don't see that happening too soon." Cody had been denying any intention of getting married for years, yet everyone seemed to push him in that direction. Not just the women either. The men rode his ass about it, but he would not give in.

"You'll fall in love, and then look out. She'll have you wrapped around her little finger." Henry's big grin irritated more than convinced him, but he thought he hid his sour attitude well behind the smile.

"I'll take your word for it, Henry."

The older man wandered off, calling over his shoulder. "Who knows. Maybe Santa will bring you a cute little beauty you can't resist."

Yeah, Cody would have one of those all right, but she

would last for the night, maybe two, and then she needed to be on her way. Then again, he never brought women to the ranch. He convinced them to take him home. He slept with them and left in the morning. That's how it always was and how it would continue to be.

After lunch, he hopped back into his truck to drive to Huntsford, the closest town, for supplies. He checked the list he'd made in his palm. The hardware store was the first on the list. Not like it wasn't always, even if he didn't need anything. The hours spent mulling over various tools was the best time of the day. After that would be what he didn't relish, which was grocery shopping. Maybe he *should* get a wife.

No way!

He drove to the end of the property and stopped to lean across the seat to open the passenger door. Macaulay jumped in, wagging his tail. "Okay, boy, you can go, but remember it's a leash in the hardware store. The only reason they let you in there is because they started selling dog food." His five-year-old black lab barked once, and Cody shook his head.

They pulled out. The long stretch of road leading to Huntsford was boring most of the way with nothing to see except ranch or farmland. A few trees dotted the landscape, fencing, a farmhouse here and there, and mountains in the distance. What grass that wasn't dead from the frigid temperatures was covered in snow from the night before. At least the sky cleared today, and the forecast hadn't predicted more snow for another week at least. They were frequently wrong, though.

Macaulay barked, and Cody lowered his window a little. His dog pushed his nose out the gap and whined. Cody scratched his head with one hand on the steering wheel. "Calm down. You're the one that insisted on coming along. If you wanted to rip and run all over the place, you should have stayed home."

Macaulay continued to whine, but Cody ignored him and drove on. At the hardware store, they wandered around, Cody content to plan building projects in his head. He did light repair like a fence or a board here and there on the ranch, but serious construction wasn't necessary. Beau had run both enterprises—the cattle and the horses at Twin Falls—with efficiency. All Cody had to do was come back and take the reins of his part. In many ways he was grateful to his brother. In others, resentful. Maybe he had expected Beau to call and beg him to come back home. A sense deep inside told him no one truly needed him, but that thought could depress the hell out of anyone, so he tamped it down.

"Hey, Cody. Macaulay."

Cody stiffened and turned. "Tammie. How's it going?"

She leaned all her weight into one leg and put a hand on her hip. "I'm good. How's that twin brother of yours?"

TRESSIE LOCKWOOD

"Involved," he lied. If Tammie couldn't have him, she wanted Beau. Cody had been with her once or twice, but Tammie was clingy and word around town was she hunted a husband.

She frowned at him. "I was only asking after his health, Cody Everett. Didn't your mama teach you any manners at all?"

He felt a muscle jump in his jaw. "Let's not talk about my mama."

Macaulay tugged at the leash. His dog hated being tied down. Must be like his owner, he guessed. Cody clicked his tongue and gave a sharp command. The dog stilled. "If you'll excuse me—"

"Why don't we go see that new movie that came out last week?" Tammie stepped closer to him and laid a hand on his chest. She peered up at him with wide blue eyes. "You can buy me dinner, and I'll..."

Open your legs. The thought of how cheap she was turned him off while he'd been sniffing around her not long ago.

"I'm sorry. I still have a lot to do to make sure the ranch is running smoothly. Too busy right now to date."

"Not too busy to see Sherrie last night," she snapped.

The fact that word had gotten around didn't surprise him, nor did he care. "Have a nice day."

He bought a few items he didn't need and left the store, then continued with the rest of his errands. When he stopped at the grocery store, he left Macaulay with a friend in his shop to keep warm. Afterward, he and Macaulay headed back along the lonely road to Twin Falls.

In the same spot where he'd barked and whined, Macaulay started up again. This time, Cody peered out over the land. A sharp decline led to a small pond, but it wasn't visible from the road. Sometimes in winter, kids skated on the surface of the water when it froze, but he knew from his own experience, it wasn't worth it because of the tiny pond size and unevenness in the ice.

He slowed down, and that's when he spotted the skid marks in the slush. Tire treads led over the side. His heart hammered in his chest, and Cody pulled to the side of the road and opened his door. Macaulay jetted past him and ran over the slope. Cody followed and stopped cold at the sight.

A black sedan lay on its side, the driver side having cracked the surface of the pond. Cody slid down the incline. He had spent hours in town, but Macaulay whined to stop here on the way in.

While he waded through the freezing water, he chided himself for not listening to Macaulay the first time. Still, there was no telling how long ago the accident happened. He just prayed he wasn't too late.

The climb to the top of the car to reach the passenger door took forever, partly because his boots and jeans were now weighted down. He felt his energy lagging because he had started to freeze. Twice he lost his footing and fell, but he kept going. When he drew up to the window, he pressed a hand to the cold glass to block out the light and tried not to fog it over with his breath. Peering inside, he made out two people. Neither moved.

"Damn it." He debated going back to get his phone to call for help, but that might take too long.

At his words, the woman stirred and opened big, brown eyes. Something shifted inside Cody, but he focused on the situation at hand. The woman began to look around, but he tapped the window. He needed her focused on him.

"Look at me, sweetheart," he called out through the window. "No, don't try to take off your seatbelt. Wait until I get you. Can you reach the lock?"

Confusion clouded her beautiful eyes, but he kept talking to her, wondering if he would end up having to break the back window. That would come with the risk of injuring her, that last thing he wanted to do.

The woman managed to click the lock, and he slid over the back door to try getting the front one open. Working against gravity with his hands freezing, he used all his strength. After more maneuvering, he held the door open with one foot and reached between his legs for her.

"Jeff," she murmured. She started to turn her head toward the driver side, but he touched her chin and kept her looking at him.

Nobody's Lover

"What's your name, honey?"

She blinked at him as if she wasn't sure. Blood stained the smooth, cocoa skin on her forehead, and he wondered if the head injury caused amnesia. Then her expression cleared. "Kaleena. My name is Kaleena. My fiancé..."

Cody's stomach dropped. For just a second, he allowed his gaze to shift to the driver, a man. His head tilted completely underwater, and Cody knew from the time it took for him to slow his car, get out, and climb up here, it had been at least ten minutes, not to mention how long ago they had the wreck. This poor woman's fiancé was gone.

He got her unbuckled and took her full weight into his arms. Shoving against the door, he raised her out of the car. "Can you put your arms around my neck?"

Her movements were sluggish, but she did as he asked, and he pulled her atop the car. The entire vehicle shifted, and he froze with her tight against his chest.

"Jeff," she murmured a small voice that cut him to the core.

"Shh, it's okay. Everything's going to be okay."

Kaleena started when Macauley barked at the pond's edge. He held her tighter, feeling he breasts press into his chest. This wasn't the time to notice how soft she was or how good she smelled despite what she'd just been through. He held her still and jumped to the ground. Freezing water sloshed in his boots, and pings of pain shot up his ankles and calves on impact. He winced but waded swiftly to shore.

Once he tucked Kaleena inside his truck, he reached for his phone and called it in to the police department. Kaleena sat on the passenger seat shivering, and he reached in back to grab a blanket to wrap around her shoulders. Her wide eyes pleaded with him, but Cody didn't want to be the one to tell her. He turned to shut the door and walk around to the driver side, but she grabbed his sleeve.

"Please. We just got engaged today…"

"I'll go." Freezing his ass off, he worked his way back down to the overturned car and fought to pull Jeff's head above water. Cody's fingers were turning blue, and he couldn't feel his toes anymore. Not even CPR would bring the man back that lay trapped. His eyes stared unseeing, and his skin had turned blue. Cody swore and climbed out of the vehicle. He made it to the top of the slope on heavy legs and climbed into his truck. Kaleena watched him with her hands pressed together in her lap.

"I'm…I'm sorry, sweetheart," he began.

She shook her head. "No, that's impossible. No…No!" Tears flooded her eyes and spilled down her cheeks. He knew she was going to lose it before she began to scream. "No, he just asked me to marry him. I said yes. I told him… He gave me a ring. See? No, *please!*"

Not knowing what else to do, he pulled her onto his

lap and cradled her in his arms. Gently, he rocked her and stroked her back. "I'm sorry, so sorry."

For a long time, she shouted and cried. Her entire body shook. He thought she might be cold, so he blasted the heat and didn't let her go for a second. No words could comfort her heart, so he let it come through his hands and his arms. He held her tight because he knew it felt like she would fly apart in pieces. He knew the devastation of loss, and how ironic that she would lose the person she loved most on these icy roads the way he lost his parents. If he hadn't found her, if Macaulay hadn't barked, she would have frozen to death. The thing he knew above all else was she must wish she had died with the one she loved.

"I'm not going to let you go. I'm right here," he encouraged her. "You don't know me, but I'm here, Kaleena. Everything will be okay. In time, it's going to be okay. For now, go ahead and cry it all out. Scream if you want. I'm here."

"Jeff." The name left her lips with such agony in its tone, it tore at him. He found tissue under the dash and leaned back a little to clean her face. She didn't fight him. In fact, from the glaze in her eyes, she didn't know he was there. She sat on his lap so small, and even with red, swollen eyes and a tear-stained face, her beauty shined through.

He pushed her hair back and smoothed it down the

best way he could. He found the spot where she'd hit her head, glad the bleeding had stopped. When a buzz began in her pocket, he started, but she didn't react at all this time. He fished around in her pocket and found her cell phone. The display read "Uncle Cornell."

"It's your uncle." He held the phone out to her, but she didn't respond.

The buzzing stopped and started up again. If he were her uncle, he'd want to know immediately what happened and that she was safe. He pressed the connect button. "Hello?"

"Who is this?" came a commanding voice through he line.

"Cody Everett."

"Well, Mr. Everett, where is my niece, and why are you answering her phone?" Cody didn't miss the implication that if the man didn't like his answer, there would be trouble.

"Kaleena's here." He closed his eyes and shifted her closer to his chest. Her head dipped to his shoulder as if she had no strength to hold it up. "Sir, I'm afraid there's been an accident."

Chapter Two

"Bro, are you sure you want to deal with this?" Beau said on the phone.

Cody sighed and dragged a hand through his disordered hair. "No, I'm not, but I can't abandon her either." He glanced over to where they'd taken Kaleena. Through the gap in the curtain, he saw that she sat on the bed, head down and hugging herself. Even while the hospital staff questioned her, she didn't respond. The haunted expression in her eyes never wavered. Sure he'd like to back out and let someone else take his place in looking after her, but how could he when he'd promised her uncle.

"You seem like a level-headed young man from the sound of your voice and from what you've described to me about what happened," Cornell Morgan had said. "I'm going to trust you to take care of her until I can come for her."

"What?" Cody had declared. "You don't know me, and more importantly she doesn't. She needs you here with her now!"

"I would give anything to be there, but that's impossible for the time being. What I'm asking you is, will you take care of Kaleena until I can get there?"

Cody had argued some more, demanding to know what he did that kept him from taking a flight out of whatever hole he found himself. From what he could gather, Kaleena's uncle had a job with the government, one he wasn't at liberty to share the details about. He mentioned the word agent, and Cody guessed it was FBI or CIA. If he was on an undercover case, even Kaleena's emotional health wouldn't make his superiors release him to go to her. Once again, Cody wondered what would have happened if he wasn't there, if someone else had found her. As he reviewed the conversation, he looked over at her again. Right now, she couldn't be alone, and from what Cornell had said, she had no other family, no close friends who would be willing to be here for her now. What kind of life had she led? He knew half the town of Huntsford and had his brother Beau too. They didn't have much in the way of family, but even his hand Henry would help him if he needed it.

"Cody, you there?" Beau called over the line.

Cody shook himself. "Yeah, I'm here. Listen, I can't abandon her. Maybe it's because of how Mom and Dad died. I don't know. She needs someone, and I'm the only one here. I'll look after her until her uncle comes. Bro, I have to go. They're signaling to me. Talk to you later."

Nobody's Lover

He ended the call. When he stood up, the chill of the floor called his attention to the fact that he wore the disposable shoe covers someone had found for him. One of his men would be there soon with a change of clothing, socks, and boots. He'd been examined already for frostbite and given the all clear.

Cody tucked his phone in his pocket and approached the doctor. He ran through potential motels for Kaleena in his mind. Maybe if someone had a room for rent that might be better with less coming and going. Huntsford was a bit far for him to check on her every day what with work keeping him busy.

"How she doing, doc?" Cody asked when he drew up to the man.

Dr. Stevens took his arm and led him out of earshot of Kaleena. He tucked the clipboard in his hands under one arm and gestured while he spoke. "There's nothing wrong with her physically except for a few bruises. The bump on the head is minor, but she might have a bit of a headache. Nothing a couple of pain pills won't help. What I'm more concerned about is her mental state."

Cody looked past him at Kaleena. She really was a beauty, shoulder length hair, pouty, kissable lips, and of course her big, brown eyes. He judged her to be no more than five foot five. The top of her head barely reached his chin, and her figure was not too small but curvy with full breasts. *Stop it, you ass. She doesn't need you lusting over her at a time like this.* He focused on the doctor. "What do you mean her mental state? I know she lost her fiancé, and she's probably depressed. Who wouldn't be?"

"I'm worried about her becoming suicidal. I can't make an accurate assessment since she won't talk, but I'd feel better about someone staying with her twenty-four seven—at least for a few days. The shock will wear off, and it will be worse for her. It's too bad she has no family to be with her in this time."

Cody got the message. Kaleena could not stay in a motel or rent a room. He had to take her home with him. He ran a hand over his face and rubbed his eyes. Hitching his shoulders and rolling his neck didn't release the tension. "I'll take her home."

The doctor's eyes widened. "I didn't mean—"

"What did you mean, doc? She needs someone to look after her, doesn't she? Who else is available? Name him or her, and I'll take her to them myself."

The man hesitated. "You aren't exactly..."

Cody frowned. "If you're about to suggest I'll do something to her in her vulnerable state, I suggest you rethink those words. I've never forced myself on a woman or tricked her into sleeping with me. I don't need to."

"I would never accuse you of that."

"Get her papers in order. If you're not keeping her overnight, I'll take her now."

By the time the doctor was ready to release Kaleena,

Nobody's Lover

Cody had received his change of clothes and breathed a sigh of relief to be fully dressed and warm. He strode into the area where Kaleena waited and stopped in front of her.

"Hey, there," he started, cursing himself for the nervousness. "Are you ready to go? You'll be staying at my house for a while, if that's okay." She didn't respond or look up. Someone had taken her boots off, so he bent to put them on. He noticed they were cut for style as much as warmth, being black suede with medium high heels. They came up over her knees, and he averted his gaze from her thighs as he zipped them. "Stand up," he ordered gently but with firmness.

She did as he asked, and she stuck her arm into her coat while he held it for her. He didn't require her to button on her own. The sooner they left this place, a reminder of what happened that day, the better. Besides, it was getting late, and he didn't want to leave Macaulay with his friend too long. He would need to stretch his legs and get something to eat.

When they pulled up to the house, Cody turned off the engine to his truck. "Let's go inside, Kaleena. I'll show you to your room."

He stepped out of the vehicle and walked around ahead of her. He strained his ears for any sign she would follow, and he blew out a breath when she opened the door and walked behind him to the house. Cody knew how to combat depression, or at least how he had done it after he left home. He moved, he did. He would not push Kaleena too hard, but he wouldn't let her lie still and get lost inside her head either. He considered what the doctor told him. Things might get a lot worse when the shock wore off. He would just have to bear down and deal with it.

He took her inside the house and headed down the hall to the room he would give her, the one next to his. That way he stood a chance of hearing if she had a rough night. When he opened the door to the room, he took in the bland furnishings, all brown wood and no fancy accents. That was because no woman had ever been in his house. He'd had it built after taking over the cattle side of Twin Falls Ranch. No, that wasn't accurate. There was the one time he'd taken it into his head to hire a maid. Her changes had irritated the hell out of him, so he'd let her go and handled things himself.

"It's not much, but it'll do for the time you're here."

She walked past him and stopped at the end of the bed. "You don't have Christmas decorations."

His eyes widened at the unexpected comment. "In here?"

"At all."

He scratched the back of his head. "I'm sorry. My brother and I don't really celebrate it." The holiday was just a couple weeks away.

"I'm glad."

Nobody's Lover

He watched as she twisted the ring on her finger. He guessed there'd been a lot of love there. *Who wouldn't love her?* He shook his head to dislodge foolish thoughts. "Are you hungry? I can microwave something or fix some scrambled eggs. Sorry, I'm not much of a cook."

"I just want to sleep if that's okay."

He nodded and turned to leave. At the door, he hesitated, but she sat on the side of the bed and began removing her boots. He scanned the room one last time and then shut the door.

* * * *

Cody opened his eyes and looked at the clock on his nightstand. Two a.m. He rubbed his temples. A headache pounded at his head, and he wondered why he woke up. Usually, he slept well throughout the night, too exhausted from the physical labor. Then he remembered Kaleena and sat up. That's what awakened him, a sound from the hall. He hurried to the door and threw it open. Kaleena was sick in the bathroom.

"Kaleena, are you okay?" he called out to her. She didn't answer, so he checked the knob. She hadn't put on the lock, but he hesitated. With no clothes to wear, he'd needed to give her something of his. He recalled how she looked in one of his T-shirts, her bare legs and feet uncovered. "I'm coming in."

20

She crouched over the commode throwing up, and he hurried to her side to pull her hair back. Tears wet her face as she dry-heaved. She'd refused any food.

"It's okay." He rubbed her back, feeling awkward again.

After some time, she struggled to her feet, and he helped her. He stayed by while she washed her mouth and wet a cloth to cool her heated face. When she stumbled turning toward the door, he put an arm around her shoulders and led her to her room.

"I'll make you tea," he offered. He didn't drink the stuff, but he was pretty sure there was some left over from the maid. Coming back in the room, he noticed she'd curled up on the bed with the covers drawn to her neck and her knees to her chest. He sat down beside her. "I didn't add sugar yet, so tell me when."

She murmured something, so he took that as enough and handed her the cup. Her hands shook.

"I'll help you." He took up a spoonful of the hot liquid, blew to cool it, and guided it between her lips. She drank in silence, trusting him not to burn her.

"Why are you doing this?"

"My mother believed tea cures all ills."

She lowered her sad gaze to the blanket and worried the ends. "Not that."

"I'm taking care of you because your uncle asked me to."

"Th-that's what I thought." She sniffed. "Uncle Cornell works with the FBI. I think he's on a case they spent a long time putting together. They can't let him go…" Her words drifted off, and she began struggling to breathe. Cody set the cup aside and nipped her onto his lap. He held her tight and tucked her face into the crook between his neck and shoulder. She gripped his forearm, her nails digging into his skin, but the movement seemed to help her calm down. "I shouldn't let you hold me."

"Take from it what you need. Nothing else matters."

"He asked me to marry him. Jeff did." She took the tissue he offered and wiped her nose. Then she climbed off his lap to curl under the covers again. "His parents hate me because I'm black. Neither of us gave a damn. We were going to get married on Christmas Day to make it extra special. We didn't need any fancy ceremony or elaborate plans."

Cody cursed. Way to ruin her Christmas forever. For the first time, he was glad for his and Beau's hang-ups. He handed out bonuses and gave his people time off, but that was as far as the celebration of the season went.

"You don't have to worry about seeing decorations here. Beau and I haven't celebrated in a long time."

"Beau?"

"My twin brother. We're mirror identical twins."

Most people exclaimed over that fact and asked stupid

questions such as if they'd traded places as kids. Kaleena gave no indication of having heard him or being impressed. He didn't blame her.

"I won't get in your way, and I'm not going to kill myself. No matter what that doctor said." Her voice wobbled on the end of the statement, so he couldn't say he believed her.

"Here, drink the rest of this tea. It will settle your stomach. I can fix you a PB&J sandwich too, if you like. You should eat something."

She frowned.

"Well...egg..."

"I'm not hungry. Thank you." She scooted down in the bed and rolled over with her back to him.

Cody gathered up the tea things and returned them to the kitchen. He made it to his bedroom door when he heard her crying. The anguish ripped through him, and he touched the door panel with his forehead, eyes shut. In a few hours, he would need to rise for the day's work, and his head still pounded. He spun on his heel and returned to her room. She didn't move or stop crying when he pulled the covers back and settled into the bed behind her. Careful not to move too close, he stroked her hair and squeezed her shoulder. "I'm here."

To his surprise, she flipped over and threw herself into his arms. He drew her to his chest, ignoring the fact that he wore no shirt, and she didn't have a bra on beneath the tee he'd given her. For a long time, she sobbed, but eventually she dropped off to sleep. From sheer exhaustion, he soon joined her.

Chapter Three

Kaleena felt him long before she came fully awake. She heard his soft breathing as he slept and felt his chest rise and fall against her breasts. Guilt assailed her for finding solace in this stranger's arms, but she had nothing else. Jeff had meant everything to her. She'd met him after years of dating losers, and at first he'd seemed too good to be true. The first man with everything going for him, including looks and a successful career, and he loved *her*. Now he was gone, and it seemed like she was cursed, that no one decent would ever come along and stay.

Every breath hurt to draw in, and thoughts tormented her because they centered around the one man aside from her uncle she loved more than life. She'd told Cody suicide didn't enter her mind, but the truth was if death came, she would welcome it. To live burned like hell, and right after she knew Jeff was gone, only Cody's voice kept her sane. He talked to her, rubbed her back, and stroked her hair. He said it would be okay, and she wanted to shout at him and tell him how stupid and empty those words were. Yet, something in them helped all the same.

Nobody's Lover

She told herself she could make it another minute, another second, since Cody went so far to help.

Somewhere nearby, a rooster crowed, and she heard the call of cattle as they stirred. A horse neighed, and out the window over Cody's shoulder, she caught sight of the skyline as it lightened. Morning always came, even when one didn't want it to. She moved a little and realized Cody's arm was slung over her side. They'd slept in the bed together all night. Guilt rose, and she pushed at his chest.

"Let me go."

He jerked away and scanned the room before jumping to his feet with a curse. "Damn it, I'm late." He crossed to the door in two long strides. Tall, she noted with little interest, maybe six foot four, and built broad-shouldered. Jeff had been big. She swallowed back tears. Cody stopped at the door. "You can sleep in today. I'll make you breakfast before I go out."

She didn't respond. Why did it seem like he emphasized "today"? Would he make her earn her keep? He wasn't such a good guy after all. In fact, what did she know about him? He might have slept in the bed with her with intentions of taking advantage of her.

He left, and she lay there. Time passed, but she didn't know how much. He came in with a tray and left it by the bed. When he paused and put a hand up, she thought he would touch her, but he drew it back. She stared at him in silence.

Why should she care if he smelled good? He did, like a fresh shower and soap. He said something, but the thoughts in her mind were too loud. She shut her eyes and rolled to her side. Hopefully, he would be gone by the time she woke up again—*if* she did.

* * * *

An earthquake jarred Kaleena from her sleep. Her covers fell away, and a chill in the air raised goose bumps on her bare legs. She shivered and moaned in fear. When the cobwebs left her head, she realized it wasn't a natural disaster but a man-made one. Cody tore away her covers and forced her to sit up. She glared at him.

"Leave me alone."

"To wallow in your pain?"

"My fiancé just died, you insensitive ass!" Saying the words unsettled her stomach. She'd been lying in bed for the last two days, sleeping off and on, eating not at all. Each night when she gave into sobs, Cody came to her and held her. His strong embrace seemed to hold the pieces of her mind together when it felt like they would fly apart. She let him hold her because the alternative went beyond reason.

"I let you stay in for two days when I'd told you one. You haven't eaten, and you haven't showered."

She put her hands on her hips, but every limb trembled

in weakness. "Are you saying I stink, because if you are, you might as well say it plain to my face."

She thought she saw amusement in his eyes before it disappeared. He stood up from the side of the bed and faced her. "I'm saying you have until the count of ten to get up and get showered and put clothes on. If you don't start by the time I reach one, I will be dumping you in the shower myself and dressing you."

Kaleena's mouth fell open.

"Ten."

"I hate you!" The damn tears filled her eyes and spilled over. She swiped a hand over her face.

"Nine."

She slid to the end of the bed and stood up. "Get out. I'm not changing while you're here."

He moved to the door and gave her a look that said he would be back if he thought she made no progress. If Kaleena had the energy or the will, she'd flip him off. Instead she scanned the room for her clothes. She thought she remembered Cody saying he had brought her things from the wreck.

A cry tore from her chest, and she sank on the bed. What about the funeral or informing Jeff's parents. She'd thought of none of that. "Oh no. I can't…"

Cody appeared in the doorway some minutes later.

She peered up at him. "I forgot about taking care of things."

He walked over and sat down beside her. When he took her hand, she tried to pull away, but he held on and rubbed a thumb over her skin where he held it. "Everything is arranged. His parents took care of it when the police department notified them. I'm sorry, sweetheart. I asked if they wanted to see you or since you know them and not me if they wanted to bring you to their house, and—"

"Don't say it." She squeezed her eyes shut, drawing in shallow breaths. "They hated the fact that he was involved with a black woman. They accused me of being after his money. I have a right to be there!"

"And you will."

She opened her eyes. "What?"

"I managed to get the information on the funeral. It will be held tomorrow afternoon. Today, you and I are going into Huntsford so you can buy a dress and if you don't have them, shoes. I'm driving you to the funeral tomorrow and staying with you. Afterward, we'll come back here."

"Why are you doing all this for me?"

"You asked me that before."

She crossed her arms over her chest. "And I can't believe it's just because there's no one else or because my uncle asked you to."

He grinned, but for the first time, she noted the sadness in his green eyes. "Well he does work for the FBI.

Nobody's Lover

I mean I don't want to suddenly be on American's Most Wanted list 'accidentally.'"

"Uncle Cornell would never do that!"

"I was kidding." He stood up. "Anyway, I'd like to leave at ten, but I want you to eat breakfast first. Twenty minutes should do it?"

She had the feeling he would be back if she didn't give in. "Fine."

Twenty-five minutes later, she'd showered and dressed. Cody's boots sounded in the hall, and she sighed at her bland countenance in the mirror. Some of her things had been ruined in the accident, and her makeup bag happened to be one of them. Not that she felt up to fixing her face. At least she'd pulled a comb through her hair. The last couple of days she didn't care that she looked a hot mess.

They sat across from each other at the kitchen table. She kept her head down, not wanting to talk as she forced herself to eat the bacon if not the eggs. This was the only meal the man knew how to make aside from peanut butter and jelly. He must think it was a healthier choice than microwave meals.

"You can't cook." She peered up at him between her lashes, and he flushed. His brows lowered, making him appear more angry than embarrassed.

"Sorry."

"It doesn't matter."

TRESSIE LOCKWOOD

They left for town when she made it clear she would not eat the eggs. He grumbled something under his breath and dumped her plate. In the passenger seat of his truck, Kaleena grabbed the door handle until her fingers hurt. She panted and tried to calm down.

"It's too soon," he said. "You can stay here and tell me your size. I'll buy your dress."

"I don't need to be babied. I'm a strong woman."

"I know you are."

Tempted to shout at him for no reason, she bit her tongue and shut her eyes. The emotions would not win. If she cried now, he would pull her onto his lap, and coddle her. She had to learn to stand by herself. The bacon lay like a stone in her stomach.

"He…" Saying Jeff's name would undo everything she vowed. "He deserves more than just a hastily picked dress by a stranger."

"I understand."

Cody turned over the engine and pulled down the drive, which was plowed clean. When they reached the road, snow and ice crunched beneath the tires, and her stomach somersaulted. Jeff had lived in Wyoming all his life, but she was from Baltimore. She didn't know the area around Huntsford at all, but an inability to forget the nightmare that ruined her life, told her when Cody drove along the stretch of road where the accident happened. She began to shake, and no amount of holding on to the armrest eased her panic.

Nobody's Lover

"Hey, I'm not familiar with the town where they're having the funeral." Cody reached in front of her to the glove compartment. "Mind checking this map over for the route there?"

Kaleena stared at the map. She had no idea where Huntsford was. The place was not a major city like Cheyenne. "Don't you have GPS?"

"It's broken." She looked at him and saw the lie in his eyes. He tapped the map. "Please. Thanks."

She knew what he was doing. He tried to distract her from taking in her surroundings and knowing just when they passed the spot. The map gave her a point to focus on, and she took the out, studying it as if it held the mystery of life. When she had at last located Huntsford, she was about to confirm the town where the funeral would take place as that of her almost in-laws, but he pulled the map from her fingers.

"Just remembered I bought a new GPS. Thanks anyway."

Kaleena glared at him and turned to the road. They were just passing a sign that read Welcome to Hunstford.

Above the main street driving in, wreaths hung on the wires at every intersection. Lights decorated the poles, but weren't turned on yet. Even in the square across from a building that must be City Hall, each tree had been decorated in celebration of Christmas. Kaleena averted her eyes, and Cody swore. He turned off from that street

32

to another called Pine Alley. Shops lined the narrow road from beginning to end. The one at the start appeared bigger than the rest, and the sign on it read Joey's Cowboy Bar. Atop the roof was a neon contraption of a cowboy riding a bull.

Cody caught her looking at it. "I sometimes go there, among other bars, for a drink. We can go together whenever you like."

"I'll pass. Thanks. You can go without me."

He parked the car, and they got out to head to the second largest building she'd spotted—the clothing outlet. They walked inside together, and Kaleena stopped to examine the signs hanging from the ceiling for the women's section.

"Cody Everett, what are you doing in here?"

Kaleena turned to see a blonde wearing a long fur coat that hung open, revealing her low cut sweater and skin tight blue jeans. She strode up to Cody and pressed close. Her upturned face was a clear invite for a kiss, but Cody frowned. "Mandy."

"Haven't seen you at Joey's lately. We miss you." She pouted prettily at him. Kaleena spun away and started walking toward the middle of the store. Maybe she would find the section easier.

"This way." Cody grabbed her arm and tugged her to the right. She didn't know he had followed but fell into step with him.

Nobody's Lover

"Cody! Fancy running into you here." Another beautiful woman with boobs ready to spill out of her blouse. Kaleena glanced at Cody. This time he didn't do more than nod and stepped around the woman, hauling Kaleena along with him.

"Old friends," he grunted.

"Not my concern." She stopped in front of a rack of dresses and began pushing them aside as she searched for a decent black one. Were they ex-lovers? Of course they were—or current ones. Maybe he moved so fast because one didn't know about the other. She had dated men like that, and they were always caught out eventually. Peering at Cody from the corner of her eye, she would have thought he wasn't that type of man, not with the way he treated her. Although she suspected his motives at first, he hadn't tried anything with her once. Then again, he might not find black women attractive, so he felt safe. That was good because she would not ever be in the market for another man and definitely not days after the loss of her fiancé.

Another woman strode up, an older one, and Kaleena cringed.

"Not *her*," Cody almost shouted. Kaleena came close to smiling.

"Hello, folks," the woman said with too much cheer. She wore a green turtleneck and a red vest over black jeans. The green boots were too much, but with the Santa hat on her head, Kaleena got what she attempted with the getup. "Just wanted to invite you to the festivities we have going on tonight. We'll have hot cocoa and eggnog, some Christmas cookies, and plenty of caroling. Our local kiddies will perform a play of the First Christmas. So come on out and have fun with us. We guarantee you'll have a good time."

She held out a flyer to Kaleena, but Kaleena couldn't raise her hand. She couldn't move at all. Cody passed in front of her, blocking the woman from view. His arm brushed her shoulder, filling her nostrils with his now familiar scent. While he spoke to the woman, blood rushed in Kaleena's ears so she couldn't hear the words. She managed to grab onto Cody's coat sleeve and just held on with both hands.

After some time, the scrape of metal on metal penetrated her haze. Cody turned and held up a dress to her. "This one is nice."

She focused. "If I was ninety-five."

Again, she recognized what he'd done for her. He knew the beast of a dress was ugly, but he'd chosen it to pull her out of the pit she'd fallen into. She moved in front of him to begin searching herself with sluggish movements.

"Thank you," she whispered.

He nodded in silence.

Nobody's Lover

* * * *

Kaleena walked into the church with Cody at her side and stopped. The casket was positioned dead center at the front. Over the heads of the other people there to pay their respects, she spotted Jeff's parents. They sat on the front row, his mother's head bowed, a tissue to her nose. Kaleena clenched her hands together. She should have brought some tissue even though she'd told herself no more tears.

"I can stand out in the lobby if you prefer and wait for you," Cody offered.

Her eyes widened, and she snagged his hand. "No! I mean, um, if you don't mind coming in…"

"Of course."

Why was he so good to her when she was a stranger? She leaned on him, and she didn't mean to, but the little strength left in her at that moment was reserved for existing.

They walked down the aisle. She felt Cody pause at the fifth or sixth row at a spot with two openings, but she kept moving. At the front, she started toward a spot a few people down from Jeff's parents. A man appeared in front of her, blocking her advance with a hand up.

"I'm sorry, folks," he whispered. "This row and the second one is reserved for family only. If you like I can show you to—"

"I am his fiancé," Kaleena interrupted. "I think I deserve to say good-bye to him on the front row. Would you like to argue about it, or should I find my seat?"

The reproving glance from Jeff's father hurt, just like it did all the times he and his wife accused her of being a gold digger. Her uncle had raised her to be honest and, hard-working, but that meant nothing in these people's eyes. Either way, she would not kowtow to them or anyone else here.

The man seemed about to say something else when Cody dropped a hand on his shoulder and smiled. "Thanks, that's all." Even she shivered because the smile wasn't the least bit friendly. The man paled, nodded, and scurried off. Kaleena sat down with Cody beside her. Whispers erupted from every direction, but she held her head up high. In her lap, her hands shook, and Cody laid one of his over hers. She welcomed his strength, which brought her through the ordeal until the last prayer was offered up on Jeff's and his family's behalf.

Chapter Four

Christmas day came and went, a day like any other if it weren't for the pain in Kaleena's heart. She sat with Cody in his living room playing cards while snow fell outside the window and a fire crackled in the hearth. Forgetting what game they played, she discarded and plucked a new card at random times, even in the middle of Cody's turn. He never complained.

"Would you like to talk?" he asked. "You know…about *him*?"

"No."

"It might help."

"You have something that has hurt you, too, and you won't tell me what it is."

He frowned and paused in the act of rearranging his hand. "That's because I think knowing my issue will hurt you more."

"You're obviously a player, but you come off to me as different. I bet everyone in this area is wondering what's gotten into you. Why hasn't your brother come over all this time? Didn't you say he lives on this ranch in his own home?"

He shrugged.

"Cody."

She thought she saw a flash of pleasure in his features, but it dissipated as swiftly as it appeared. Who knew what could have made him happy at that second, but she found for the first time she could look past her own pain and be glad he'd experienced that small glimmer. For all he'd done on her behalf, it was the least he deserved.

"Thank you so much for helping me through this difficult time." She hated how stiff she sounded, like a boring greeting card. "I wouldn't have made it without you."

He nodded.

Kaleena's cell phone rang, and she started since it had stayed silent for the most of the time she'd been there. She checked the display, happy to see her uncle's name flash on the screen.

"Uncle Cornell."

"Hey, kitten, how are you doing? You sound better than the last time I spoke to you."

"I'm all right."

"Is he treating you well? I don't want to have to shoot him."

She managed a half smile but let it fall when she realized her uncle couldn't see it. "He's been good to me. I'm thankful it was Cody who found me."

"Good. Well, I'm flying in tomorrow to get you. Will you be ready to go?"

Nobody's Lover

She looked at Cody. His dark head was bowed as he shuffled all the cards together. She hadn't thought their game ended. For some reason, a new sense of loss washed over her at the prospect of leaving him. Putting it down to the kindness he'd shown and the peace she found in his home, she answered her uncle. "Yes, I'm ready."

Cody's head popped up, his eyebrows raised in question. Kaleena got all the details of her uncle's flight and the time, and then she ended the call. She bit her lip, fiddling with the phone. "He's coming for me tomorrow morning. Um, I know I've been in your way here, so if you don't mind taking me to the airport, we can just get a flight out right away."

"You do not have to fly out right away. I have room here for both of you."

"No, I think it's best." She sighed and rose to her feet. "The sooner I put Wyoming out of sight the better. I want to get back to my life and try to heal. I will never forget what you did for me, and I hope somehow if I can't repay you for your kindness that someone else will."

"Enough with the thanks." He seemed grumpy all of a sudden, but she didn't know why. He stood up and touched her cheek. "Taking care of a beautiful woman is no hassle for me and wouldn't be for any man."

She swayed toward him and then checked herself in embarrassment. Spinning on heel, she rushed from the room to go get packed. What little she had wouldn't take so long, but she needed to be alone. More loneliness would await her back home, and she would have to begin job hunting, since she'd left her last position to live here with Jeff.

The day dragged on, but she and Cody figured out how to keep each other busy to get through it. They played endless games, and she even joined him outside in the cold to shovel snow off the front and along the walkways that led to various buildings. She watched him feed his cattle in the afternoon and let him persuade her to fork a few piles of hay herself. Being a city girl, the scent of the animals was strong, but she endured it without complaint.

By the next morning, she rose and took a shower, then dressed. Lugging her bag down the hall, she ran into Cody, and he grabbed it from her, lifting it with ease. She followed behind him.

"Do you want to grab some breakfast?" he offered.

"You mean out?"

He stopped and turned, running his free hand through his hair. "Sorry for forcing you to eat my cooking all week."

She stepped closer to him, and his brows rose toward his hairline. From the time she laid down in bed last night, she'd planned to thank him in the best way she knew how. With her hands on his chest, she stood on her toes and pressed her lips to his. While she knew what she intended, surprise shot through her anyway—and something else—when their mouths touched.

She would have ended the kiss there, but Cody dropped her bag and wrapped his arms around her. He drew her into a tighter embrace and tilted his head to the side. He parted her lips, and for a moment she panicked thinking he would stick his tongue into her mouth, but he didn't. Their lips locked together for too long. She struggled in his arms and pushed at him. At last, he got the message and let go.

"I apologize."

Kaleena touched her lips and turned away. The same guilt that plagued her from day one hit, because she liked the kiss. "It was my fault. I shouldn't have started that. I just wanted to show you how grateful I am. Thank you."

The leather of her bag crackled as he squeezed it. "Let's get going."

"Okay."

At the airport, their wait lasted only half an hour before her uncle arrived. He pulled her into his arms for a comforting hug, and she sighed laying her head on his shoulder. Uncle Cornell had raised her from a newborn when her mother died from the complications of childbirth. She'd never known her father.

"How are you, kitten?" Uncle Cornell asked.

She shrugged.

He kissed the top of her head. "I'm so sorry. If I could

take this all back, I would."

"I know."

He kept her close and turned to Cody, holding out his hand. "And thank you for taking care of my niece. I'm glad to meet the man who took on my responsibility so readily. I greatly appreciate it." Cody shook his hand. Kaleena watched him, noticing the color in his face, but Cody stood tall and confident. He met Uncle Cornell's gaze without wavering. She'd seen many men cower in front of him, especially knowing of his high-powered job. Uncle Cornell pulled his wallet from his pocket. "Let me compensate you for whatever expenses Kaleena incurred."

Cody frowned. "That won't be necessary." He looked at her. "I hope she finds happiness again because she more than deserves it. Kaleena, it was great meeting you. Good luck."

Before she could respond, he nodded to her uncle again and then turned to walk away. Kaleena stared after him until the crowd in the busy airport swallowed him up. When she focused on her uncle, she found him watching her with a curious expression.

"What?"

He shook his head. "Nothing. Let's get going."

* * * *

Nobody's Lover

One year later…

"Uncle Cornell, I've made a decision," Kaleena told her uncle.

He didn't raise his head from the plate of eggs, pancakes, and sausage she'd made him. He wolfed most of it down in a few bites and sipped hot coffee around studying the newspaper. Who read the newspaper anymore?

"What's that, kitten?"

"I'm going to Wyoming."

That got his attention. "Why?"

She straightened in her chair and raised her chin. "I'm going to make new, happier memories with Cody."

"And have you discussed this with him?"

"No, but I know he went through something that helped him know where I was coming from with my grief, but he wouldn't share it. He said he never celebrates Christmas, and neither does his brother. I didn't get the sense that it was a religious thing, so I'm going out there to help him, like he helped me."

The doubt in her uncle's expression frustrated her because she knew she took a big risk even doing this. What if Cody had a woman by now? What if he slammed the door in her face or told her to go home? Uncle Cornell voiced all of these worries, but she refuted each one.

"He was a player when I was there. I know he didn't

take women seriously, and I'm not going there to be his girlfriend or his lover."

"Are we that close we can discuss your love life, Kaleena?"

She smirked. "Yes, we are. And I'm telling you, that's not why I'm going. He saved my life. I told you everything on the plane ride back. I think the fact that I was able to smile and laugh again is because of him. It's only been a year and I'm not looking to try a relationship, but as Cody's friend, I want to help him laugh and enjoy this time of year. I want to rebuild it for myself too. I don't want to wallow in sadness every Christmas from now on. I want joy and happiness as the carols say. So whether it's smart or stupid, I'm going. I thought I'd just let you know."

He folded the paper and set it aside. "Then good luck. If he is rude to you, I will shoot him."

Kaleena rolled her eyes and laughed. "Thanks, Uncle Cornell. I'm going to make my flight reservations. Just leave your dishes in the sink, and I'll wash them when I come back downstairs. I love you."

"I love you too. Enjoy Wyoming."

"I definitely will."

She made her plans quickly, and before she knew it her plane touched down at her destination. Excitement brewed in her stomach at seeing Cody again. Not because she had feelings for him—although she couldn't deny there had been an awareness of him as a man that caused her guilt back then. The real reason was because he deserved to be happy. His sweetness when he looked after her told her he had a good heart. People like that tended to be hit harder by life's trials. Hell, she'd felt like she wouldn't come back into the light of day after losing Jeff, and sometimes it still felt that way. Hope she attributed to Cody kept her going forward, and she would offer him the same, even if she had to drag his ass out of the house to sing carols at the community gathering.

Oh to see his face when I suggest it. She smiled to herself and went to make arrangements for a ride out to Twin Falls Ranch. A stopover at the outlet store, and soon Kaleena arrived at Cody's door. In the early evening, she caught sight of a couple ranch hands but not Cody, and she paid the driver, having him set her things on the porch.

Taking a deep breath, she knocked and waited.

"Uh, excuse me?"

She froze and then turned around, spotting a young woman with a very pregnant belly over toward the side of the house. Panic set into Kaleena. She swallowed. Had he not only found someone special but gotten her pregnant too? What would the woman think of her showing up unannounced without a call?

"Um-uh, hi," she stuttered. "Maybe I'm at the wrong house." She felt like an idiot and knew she had the right place. The ranch had a feeling of coming home even if she'd spent just a few days there. A sense of pain and loss also washed over her, but she refused to give into it. Her time with Cody, his kindness, needed to be the focus.

"If you're looking for Cody, I think he's in one of the buildings out back," the woman said.

"I—"

"I'll go get him."

She disappeared before Kaleena could tell her never mind. She looked down at herself and what she wore, along with all the packages and her luggage. He would think she was a psycho stalker. He'd toss her on the next plane out of the state and tell her not to return.

No. Calm down, Kaleena. This isn't that big a deal. If he had a woman, she'd deal with it—embarrassed as hell—and then go home. Besides, it wasn't like she'd come to get with him anyway. She came as a friend and nothing more.

Cody must have come in through the back door because she heard boots on the hardwood floor coming closer. All Kaleena's bravery drained away in an instant when the door swung wide and there he stood. Damn, how had she not remembered how sexy he was? No, she recalled all right. The times she'd cried in his arms were ingrained in her head, even if she couldn't appreciate back then how it felt.

She perked up and smiled. "Merry Christmas. I'm

47

here for a visit. Do you remember me?"

"Kaleena."

That he pronounced her name with a hint of pain must be her imagination. She held her arms out to the sides and spun. "See? I'm going to be your elf." She'd worn an outfit similar to the woman's at the outlet store that time last year, but hers included bootie-type shoes, curled at the toes. She'd waited until they were on the way to the ranch to slip into them. "Well?"

He frowned. "You're going to catch a cold. Where is your coat?"

"That's your response?"

"It's the only sane one."

She put her hands on her hips. "I don't remember you this grouchy."

"I held it in because you didn't need my sour attitude along with everything else you had to deal with. You already know this isn't my favorite time of year, and that day is less than a week away."

"I know, right? I almost couldn't get a flight out here. There were last minute cancellations." She turned to grab the biggest bag to drag into the house. "Well, I'm here now, so that's the important thing."

He reached past her, and in true Cody fashion, dwarfing her with his big, muscular size, he nabbed the bag from her hands, along with a few others. He left her with the lighter packages, and she followed him inside.

The grin widened. He didn't intend to leave her out in the cold.

"Will I get my usual room?"

Cody tossed her an annoyed look over his shoulder, but something told her he was less upset with her showing up out of the blue than he put on. He walked down the hall to her previous room and set her bags by the bed. She dumped the rest of the things on the mattress and glanced around. "This place didn't get any more cheery since I've been gone." She hesitated. "That pregnant woman I saw out front..."

"Henry's wife."

She just managed to cut off the sigh of relief. "Oh, okay. I didn't remember seeing her before." His ranch hand had married a younger woman. She guessed them to be about ten years apart in age. Good for him.

Cody studied her, and she shifted from one foot to the other under his intense gaze. "You've grown stronger. You seem happier."

She smiled. "Thanks. I intend to be."

"What are you doing here?" He stuffed his hands in his jeans pockets, and she recalled how they had stroked her back on many occasions. A desire for him to stroke more than that took her by surprise, and she tamped down the thought.

"I'm here to celebrate Christmas with you," she announced.

Nobody's Lover

"I told you—"

"I know." She gathered up the bags from the outlet store and started past him. "We're making new memories, you and me. We're going to turn this ranch and the surrounding area into a place of joy instead of depression."

"You sound like a greeting card," he grumped. "I can do without all the cheer."

She hummed a holiday tune, ignoring him. Maybe she should go back into town and buy a CD player to blast some music in this house. No, that might drive him to strangle her. One step at a time.

In the living room, she began pulling out decorations. A row of lights around the mantel, and a wreath above it. Cody hadn't put anything on that brick wall, which was criminal in her opinion. She glanced around for a stool and then found one in the kitchen. Still humming, she climbed up and began arranging the wreath.

"Tell me when this is in the middle," she called over her shoulder.

"Kaleena!"

She smiled with her back to him. His saying her name pleased her. *Get a grip, Kaleena. Friend.* She did not want to open herself up to another relationship. General life happiness was one thing, pursuing love another. She glanced back at him standing in the doorway to the hall. He did look good in his jeans.

"Is it straight?"

He frowned at her in response, and she sighed.

"You are such a grump. Do you really want me to be sad every Christmas forever? You saw how much pain I was in last year. Can you do this for me if not for yourself?"

"To the left two inches." With that curt reply, he stalked from the room, but she'd won the battle. There would be more, but she would not give in. With the wreath in place and a few other holiday odds and ends placed, she attacked the banister out front, winding lighted garland all around it. In the windows, she tacked up lights with candles centering them. She blew up an inflatable Santa with reindeer just off the drive. From the looks of it, snow had fallen recently, and there would be more before she left no doubt. Half way through her setup, she realized she had no idea how to do the wiring and stood there frowning at everything.

"Kaleena."

She jumped, hearing Cody behind her. When she turned, she found him closer than she thought and looked up into his eyes. Had they been that green last year?

"Is part of your plan to have me take care of you again?"

"What do you mean?"

Big hands began buttoning her coat, and she stood still to let him. Some sense of feeling special came over her.

Nobody's Lover

"I'm not trying to get sick, but would you consider doing me a favor?"

He glared. She let it roll off her.

"I can't figure out how to do the wiring to light up everything at once. I bought outdoor extension cords, so that's not the problem. Do you have outdoor jacks, or will I need to run this through a window or under a door?"

"I didn't give you permission to transform my house! You can stay here as long as you like, but I have to draw the line at stupid men in a red suit and a moose."

She blinked. "Seriously? Moose? You're kidding, right?"

His face reddened, and she put her hands on his chest and extended up to her toes to kiss his cheek. "Thanks."

Cody didn't say a word as she walked into the house. The bag she'd brought to the kitchen on her way to her bedroom lay in the refrigerator, and she took this time to bring it out and unload it on the counter. She turned on the oven and searched Cody's cupboards for pans and cookware. Just as she thought, there were none. Good thing she'd picked up disposable items. If she needed more, she would ask him to take her to town and buy reusable pans and other kitchenware.

Soon she had a pan of chocolate chip cookies in the oven and one cooling on the stovetop. She made sugar cookies and peanut butter as well. Because the day had grown late, she would wait to make an elaborate meal tomorrow and definitely on Christmas Day. Tonight, she intended to feed him spaghetti with homemade meatballs and garlic bread. For dessert they would eat some of the cookies, and she would brew hot cocoa with marshmallows for them to enjoy near the fireplace.

When Kaleena stepped from the kitchen to see what Cody was up to, she spotted him outside, stomping back and forth between her lawn decorations and the lights on the porch. Santa came to life, rising as air filled him from the automatic pump. The garland twinkled all around the porch, and she clapped her hands bouncing up and down. This would be the best Christmas Cody ever had, if she had anything to say about it.

Chapter Five

"This is good," Cody said, sampling from the plate she'd handed him. She sat across from him, her legs tucked to the side on the couch and balanced her plate on one hand. Cody had dropped into a chair nearer to the fireplace and kicked his boots off. She figured he must be frozen after being outside in the snow.

"Thanks. Why does that compliment sound so grudging?"

"Your imagination."

She laughed, and he stared at her as if struck.

"What? Do I have food on my nose or something?"

He glanced away and took a huge bite of garlic bread. The way he devoured half the serving of spaghetti, she figured he wasn't flattering her saying he liked it. A warm, fuzzy feeling came over her, and she tucked into her own food.

"After this I have cookies and hot cocoa. I'm going to make enough for all of your staff to have some and extra to take home to their families."

He grumbled. "I'm sure their wives or girlfriends make their own."

"It's a gift. I bet you don't give them anything for Christmas."

The offense stood plain in his eyes. "I give them a bonus in pay without fail."

"Impersonal."

"Kaleena."

"Cody," she mocked.

His glare made her smile, and she moved to perch on the arm of his chair. She drew her feet up, sitting so close her hip and part of her ass brushed his arm. She had no idea where the boldness came from, but the flush to his handsome face pleased her. After finishing off her food, she leaned forward and placed the plate on the coffee table then sat up licking a bit of sauce from her forefinger. She started to do the same with her middle finger, but Cody's hand shot out and arrested her wrist. She blinked at him.

He held onto her and bent to place his plate on the table. To her surprise, he stuck her finger into his mouth and sucked. White-hot need shot straight down to her pussy. Her eyes widened, and she gasped. "Um..."

"Do you think you can tease me like that and get away with it?" he demanded. Green, sexy eyes full of anger and desire flashed at her.

"I didn't..."

"Don't you dare say you didn't mean to tempt me. You meant it. Your ass in those tight pants, rubbing against my arm, then bending over to give me a good view of it, what exactly did you think would happen?"

Was he pissed off? Did he intend to throw her out?

Cody jerked her from the chair arm and into his lap. She breasts bumped his chest. A low growl escaped him, and she licked her lips. He watched the movement, locked on it as if he couldn't look away. He released her wrist and rested his hands at her waist. A tug brought her even closer, and it came home real quick just how much she'd turned him on. His hard cock pushed against her ass, sending her heartbeat into overdrive.

"You need to understand what you're getting into when you so obviously offer yourself to a man like me."

The words "I'm not offering myself" rose to her lips, but who was she kidding? She wanted him. The guilt she'd felt being attracted to him, and the level of pain over the last year had lessened. If she was honest, she would admit all the talk about coming here as a friend was a lie she told herself.

She bought herself time. "So what are you saying?"

"You know exactly what I'm saying."

She ducked her head, biting her bottom lip. If she let this go forward, where would that lead them? Would she find herself hurt when it came time to go back home? Last year, it hadn't taken two seconds in town for her to realize Cody played the field. More than one woman preened in front of him, hoping he would give her the time of day.

Besides, falling in love with Cody Everett wasn't in the plan. She had one task, and that included learning to love Christmas again. Okay, now there were two—having hot sex. That too would be a memory to explore and re-explore over the next few months, maybe even years, when she slept alone with no one to love.

Kaleena hopped off Cody's lap, and he let her stand. She kept her back to him, deciding again if she would go through with this. When she reached a decision, she sank down and sat in the middle of his lap. With a small push, she ground into his cock. Cody sucked in a breath and gripped the chair's armrests.

"Kaleena, baby, you better be sure about this."

She turned and placed a knee on either side of his thighs. Leaning in close so her breasts were flush with is face, she popped open a button. "I'm sure. Do you want me?"

Another button opened and then another. His gaze dropped to her revealed cleavage. Kaleena had always liked the size of her breasts. As a C cup, she had just enough to please a man without being too much. Sure, there were other aspects of her figure she disliked, such as the extra junk in her trunk and the spreading of her hips. Over the last year, she struggled with gaining twenty pounds and losing only fifteen. Still, she didn't look bad, and from Cody's reaction, he agreed.

Her blouse hit the floor, and her pink bra with a see

through quality over the breasts caught and held Cody's gaze. Now she knew why she'd even worn the thing when she had plenty of serviceable ones that were less sexy. No matter how much she fooled herself with the reasons why she came, her subconscious knew the real deal.

Cody's hands slid up her thighs to her waist and higher to the sides of her breasts. He thumbed the beginning swell there and moaned. Leaning in, he nosed into the valley in the middle and breathed deep. "You smell incredible."

"It's my body wash." She reached back to undo the clasp on her bra, but he stopped her.

"Let me."

She waited while he undid the hooks with one hand, a practiced movement, she guessed. No getting ideas about this man. He loved women, *many* women from what she'd seen. Cody dragged the bra straps over her shoulders and down her arms, allowing her breasts to pop free.

"Damn, damn, damn," he murmured.

She shivered. The fire had died down some.

"Let me warm you, baby."

When his lips closed over her nipple, fire licked her veins, and her pussy heated. She knotted her fingers in his hair and dragged him closer while arching into his touch. His tongue curled over her flesh, teasing her nipple until it puckered. He flicked the end and then sucked it deep between his lips. She moaned at the ache he caused in such a short amount of time. Just a few hours in his presence and cookies and cocoa be damned. Having Cody inside her far outweighed the special treat.

He stood up with her in his arms and moved to the animal skin rug before the hearth. After he'd laid her down, he tossed another log on the fire and stirred it. Sparks flew, and heat engulfed Kaleena's body. She reached for her pants, but Cody was back to brush her hands aside.

"I want to discover what you have for me."

She raised her arms above her head and wiggled on the fur beneath her. Cody's gaze caressed like a touch. He pinched open the button on her pants and yanked the zipper down.

"Have you seen this?" he asked, and she glanced down at herself. He dragged her shoes off and took her pants and panties with them to toss aside. All she saw was her wide hips, thick thighs, and the tiny square of trimmed hair at her apex.

"Seen what?"

He kissed the delicate skin beneath her navel. His hands supported her ass and raised her hips for more exploration. The spots he caressed with this tongue sent new shivers through her, but not because of the chilled air. Cody's touch brought her body to life when she hadn't found the need to use her fingers for pleasure in a long while.

Nobody's Lover

He sat up and unbuttoned his shirt then pulled it off and threw it aside. His bare chest expanded firm and smooth. He slid up over her, one knee holding his weight on the floor. With a palm flattened over her pussy, he peered into her eyes. So much emotion stirred in his gaze, and she felt answering ones in her own, but she looked away. His shoulder with the reflection of lights flashing on it seemed a safer spot to focus on. Kaleena traced a finger along the skin there, and felt him shudder. She turned him on, and there was satisfaction in knowing that.

Fingers teased her soft wetness, and she gasped. He didn't dip inside like she expected him to.

"I want to be inside you." The roughness in his tone told her how far his desire had gone. She licked her lips.

"I'm not stopping you."

He leaned down and kissed her. She parted her lips and met the tip of his tongue with hers. They held off delving deep into each other's mouths. Her desire climbed to another height, and Cody tilted his head to kiss her hard. She moaned, gripping his shoulders.

When he drew back, she bit off a complaint.

"Hey."

"Hm?" she murmured.

"I know I've come this far, and trust me it's taking everything not to say fuck it and take you. I have to give you this chance, Kaleena."

She looked up at him. "What chance?"

"You're different. You know the sex life I've led. You saw a little of it last year, and that hasn't changed." When he broke eye contact, it surprised her. "Not entirely."

"What are you saying?"

He moved his hand from her pussy, and she almost sobbed. "Do you know how beautiful you are? That soft chocolate skin, those nipples. Hell the whole package. I don't think I've wanted a woman as much as I want you, and I have to admit I've never been with a black woman. Who knows if that's a factor. You're different than the others."

"Because I'm black?"

"Because you're *you*."

She said nothing.

He dropped his head and swore. His lips touched her neck, and he rose a little to knee her thighs apart. "Tell me no, Kaleena. I screwed this up big time. Baby, tell me no now because I'm about to burst out of my pants."

"I-I don't want to tell you no. I want you inside me." She ran her toes along his pants leg, lifting her leg higher. He leaned back and watched her pussy lips part. From the swirling sea green in his eyes, she knew he got off on what he saw. Her juices were flowing big time because she desired him so much. "Take me, Cody. I'm right here waiting for you."

She didn't have to ask twice. He shed the rest of his clothing in seconds, and she caught her breath at the size of his cock. Thick and long, it extended from his body as if ready to plunge inside her. Her mouth watered, and she reached down to skim it with her fingertips. Cody braced all his weight on his hip, allowing her to explore.

"Protection," she whispered, knowing she couldn't hold off much longer.

"Don't move." He rose and disappeared from the room, but he returned in seconds. Several packets rained on the floor beside her, and he selected one and tore it open with his teeth. Just how many times did he expect to go around?

Cody positioned himself between her legs, and she sat up to take the condom from him. Carefully, she rolled it onto his cock, loving how his shaft jumped and twitched at her every touch. She peered up at him while she worked, and he captured her chin to kiss her lips. Their tongues met, and she moaned in his mouth. For a long while, the only sound in the room was there hungry kisses and the crackling fire.

Cody broke their connection first and pressed her down by her shoulders. He didn't lie on top of her right away but stayed where he was, just staring. Since he liked to look, she decided to give him something to enjoy. She raised her feet off the floor and reached between her legs. Easing a finger into her wet snatch, she gasped in ecstasy, all to drive him insane. With her other hand, she stroked her breast and pinched her nipple. Her bottom lip caught between her teeth, she arched and whimpered.

"Kaleena."

In and out, she worked her finger, until her juices coated it. Cody pulled it free and stuck her digit between his lips. He licked every drop of her come away. The rumble of his moan sent chills racing from her hand to her arm and down to her core. She could tease him all she wanted, but any little movement on his part produced the same results in her.

He pressed her hands to her sides and brought the tip of his cock to her entrance. "I'm going to take it slow."

"I'm not a virgin."

"I know."

He didn't need to say it had been a while. They both knew. She shut her eyes, and her heart raced. Should she stop him? No, she couldn't now. He'd lose it. Going this far, letting another man make love to her meant no going back. Of course she knew she couldn't return to the past, but this.

"Baby."

Her fingers spasmed, and he released her wrists. She opened her eyes slowly to find Cody moving to the side. He pulled her with him and wrapped his arms around her. There had to be an end to this man's patience and his understanding. She rested her head against his chest. His cock throbbed against her belly. Before she changed her mind or he stopped her, she wrapped a leg around his waist, grabbed his cock, and pushed it between her folds. A slight ache and then pleasure assaulted her as his tool stretched her pussy.

"Don't," he groaned, obviously fighting his pleasure. "You shouldn't do anything you don't want to. In the morning, you'll only regret it." Even as he said that, he grabbed her ass and held her in place as he sank his shaft deeper.

Kaleena's jaw grew slack. She took time trying to form words. He felt good inside of her, so thick and hard. Rotating her hips, she took it all, drew back, and came in again for more. Cody rolled to his back, and she straddled him, riding for all she was worth. She braced herself with her hands on his stomach and leaned forward to feel him slide out. Then she came down hard. Pleasure erupted from all points. Her core muscles tightened. She threw her head back and rode him faster.

"Yes, oh, it feels so good," she moaned.

"Easy, my beautiful little filly," he encouraged her. "Don't hurt yourself.

"More, Cody. Please give me more!"

He lifted her off his cock and made her get on her hands and knees. When he threaded his cock into her heat from behind, she screamed his name. He held onto her hips and pounded deep. The slap of their bodies coming together heightened the enjoyment. Kaleena dropped down to stick her ass in the air. Cody took what she'd almost denied them both until an orgasm began to build. Kaleena keened and bit her lip. She reached between her legs and pinched her clit. Cody thrust harder.

"I'm not going to be able to hold this much longer," he growled.

"Let's do it together. I'm so close." She hadn't gotten the words past her lips before he took her over the edge with a powerful climax. A heartbeat after, Cody's hips jerked against hers, and he shouted his release. They pumped together for a few moments until the sensations eased. Then he pulled out. He helped her onto her side and lay behind her with his arm around her waist.

"Was that good for you, baby?"

"Hell, yes."

He chuckled, and it was the first time she'd ever heard it. His voice, so deep and sexy, made her snuggle closer to him.

"I'll take you again in a few minutes."

She sat up. "Okay, I'm going to bring cookies for you to sample." Before he could answer, she jumped to her feet and headed for the kitchen. All the way, she felt his gaze on her and decided to add a little more swing to her hips. When she returned with an assortment of the three kinds of treats she'd made, Cody lay on his back with his hands behind his head. His cock had already stiffened, and she wondered if he'd wear out her poor little kat before the night ended.

Nobody's Lover

She dropped down on the carpet beside him. "Hm, I think I had much less time than I thought."

His smile had been replaced with his usual pensive expression. "It had been a while for me as well."

She raised an eyebrow but made no comment. Discussing his love life didn't interest her. With all the women who must throw themselves at his head every time he went to town, she didn't exactly believe him.

"Peanut butter," he announced.

"Hm?"

He nodded toward the plate, which she'd set on the table.

"One can't have enough peanut butter."

She grinned and broke off a piece to feed him. When his lips touched her fingers, an arrow of desire pinged her core. She took another small piece and popped it into her mouth, then leaned down to kiss him. Just as she hoped, Cody's tongue shot out and snagged the morsel from her mouth to his. They moaned together and kissed, Cody's arms encircling her.

What did she feel for him, and why did he let her stay? Did he bring other women out here on a regular basis? She turned over to face him and ran a finger along his cheek. The silky dark hair drew her attention next, and she didn't resist running her hand through it. The man's sexiness knew no bounds and should be against the law. She scooted in closer, allowing her nipples to just graze his chest. His cock stirred between them.

Kaleena kissed his neck and trailed the caress to his shoulder. She breathed in the heady scent—all male. The glow from the fireplace lit his skin from this angle, and the smooth, taut texture drew her lips again and again.

"I get the feeling you can't keep your hands or lips off me."

She raised an eyebrow at him. "Do you want me to?"

"Never." He skimmed fingers over her back and tucked her into his embrace. "I should get covered because I'm losing the ability to wait."

"You lost that long ago. Cody?"

"Hm." His gaze dropped to her lips.

"Why don't you celebrate Christmas?"

He stiffened.

"Don't do that. I know it's something painful, but I think you know you can tell me. I went through hell, and you were there. I want you to—"

"My parents," he interrupted. "When Beau and I were eighteen, they were killed in a car accident, driving on an icy road. It was on Christmas Day."

She gasped. "Oh no! I'm so sorry. How terrible. You're legally adults at that age, but you still feel like kids, dependent on your parents to take care of you."

His expression registered surprise. "Yes, that's how it was." He stood and left the room then returned with a blanket. He sat down and patted the space in front of him as he leaned on the front of the couch. She scooted between his legs and lay on his chest while he covered them both with the blanket. "It's been sixteen years."

"So you're thirty-four?"

"Mhm."

"It must have been hard. I can't imagine the pain you must have felt. I never knew either of my parents. My mother died in childbirth, and she never mentioned my father. She didn't tell anyone his name, or I think Uncle Cornell would have looked into finding out who he was. I did dream of having a big family of my own some day, but that won't happen now."

His hold tightened for a moment. "You're..."

"Twenty-nine."

"Young enough to have babies." He stroked her belly, and she bit her lip, closing her eyes. For an instant, she imagined having a set of twins but brushed that stupid thought out of her head.

"But I'm not willing to open myself up to the kind of relationship I had with Jeff. We were soul mates."

"You believe in that?"

"You don't?" She twisted around to look into his face.

He shrugged. "I suppose I should, given my parents decided it was fate that they found this place. They believed everything about their relationship and each other was meant to be."

"How so?"

He nodded toward the back of the house as if they had a clear vision of what he referred to. "At the end of our property, where it leads up into Cloud Peak, there are hot springs. Two of them. When my dad found the place, they'd just discovered my mom was pregnant with Beau and me. They decided it was fate and called the ranch Twin Falls to represent us."

"Wow, that is so romantic. Can I see the springs?"

"If you like." He hesitated. "Some other time."

She figured out that he thought she wouldn't be able to handle it right now what with the way Jeff died. Her heart warmed at his thoughtfulness, and he might be right.

They settled into silence, and Kaleena grabbed a few more cookies. She ate the chocolate chip and fed Cody the peanut butter. Every time she held up a piece, he used it as an excuse to suck her finger along with the treat.

"Seriously?" She laughed.

"Yes, I'm very serious about how good you taste."

She trembled in delight. "Why did you let me barge in here and stay without any notice?"

"You're beautiful."

She smacked his arm. "That's it? Then any woman would do."

He shrugged again, and she resisted strangling him. Cody made it clear he would not answer any questions he didn't want to, and no amount of goading on her part would change his mind.

"Well if you're going to be like that, I'm going to clean the kitchen." She moved to stand, but he pulled her back into his arms and kissed the sensitive area behind her ear.

"No...you're not."

Chapter Six

Kaleena rushed through most of the work she had to do that day. Excitement bubbled up inside her until she felt like running through the house singing Jingle Bells at the top of her lungs. Every time the urge hit, she had to laugh at herself. One night in a man's arms, and she'd gone psycho. One would think she was the kind of woman who needed a man, but that couldn't be further from the truth. Kaleena prided herself on taking care of her own business, and until last year, she'd lived on her own, had a job, and never asked anyone for anything.

After she left Wyoming, she'd planned to start her life anew and just put one foot in front of the other until the pain eased and her joy returned. Uncle Cornell was the one to encourage her to stay with him a little longer and to work temp assignments until she felt stronger. She'd seen it as a good idea. The gung-ho plan had meant nothing without the energy, and energy was the one thing she lacked back then. At last, it appeared she'd broken free of the gloom and doom, and Christmas would be a happy time if she had to beat it into submission.

"What are you so happy about?" Cody grumbled when he entered the room where she vacuumed. Kaleena shut off the machine. Sometime in the middle of the night, Cody had carried her to bed, but he hadn't joined her. She woke up alone, and at first the depression descended like a beast. She'd fought it, and then she found new ammunition against it for her and for Cody. He on the other hand apparently lost the battle.

"I found a party," she chirped.

He cringed.

"A Christmas party!" She dug into her jeans pocket and fished for the flyer. Cody's gaze strayed to her breasts, but when he caught her watching him, he looked away. Kaleena bounced over to him. "Check this out. It's on Third and Apple. Do you know where that is?"

He frowned. "I'm familiar."

"So we can go, right?"

"I'm not going to a barn party."

Her eyes widened. "Barn? Like with animals?"

Cody seemed about to turn away and walk out of the room. She latched onto his arm and pressed close. His expression morphed from angry to questioning, but then he shifted it to indifference, one he wore too often for her liking.

"There are no animals there, and as far as I know there never were. The place is built to look like an authentic barn, all wood with a large area of floor space for dancing or tables. People rent it out for Western weddings or any other type of party. This time it happens to be a Christmas party. I'm sure they had a Halloween one in October."

"Nice! It sounds perfect. So it's at seven, and I think we should leave at six to get there on time. Do you have something good to wear?" She touched a finger to her lip, wondering if people out this way dressed up for barn parties, or if it was casual. The flyer hadn't said. She'd been thrilled to find it on the porch that morning when she stepped out to get a breath of fresh air.

"I've already said I'm not going, Kaleena. I allowed you to set up all this crap around my house, but I won't spend an entire evening pretending to be all cheery around a bunch of people doing the same thing."

"My decorations are not crap, and how do you know those people aren't happy?"

"Why would they be?"

She huffed. There was no talking to him. If she thought she could come in and snap her fingers and he'd change, she was so wrong. Cody resisted happiness like it was something evil he needed to avoid. Hanging the Christmas decorations depended on her going ahead and doing it, but she couldn't drag him out of the house, and she didn't have a ride into town.

While she stood there with the flyer in her hand, she considered what she would do. The number printed on the bottom jumped out at her, and she grabbed her cell phone from the table where she'd laid it while cleaning.

She punched in the numbers. "Hello, is this Jen, the coordinator for the Christmas party?"

"Merry Christmas, dear! Yes, this is Jen. How can I help you?"

Kaleena almost winced at the decibel level the woman decided to speak in and found herself wondering if this was one of the people Cody felt was faking it. She suppressed that thought and asked the question she needed to. "Hi, Jen. I'm calling because I was wondering if there's any chance of someone picking me up tonight."

Kaleena glanced at Cody, but he only frowned and crossed his arms over his chest as he leaned against the wall. Did he think she bluffed, or was he wondering if she intended to get someone to help convince him to come?

"Well, I'm sure we can work something out," Jen told her. "We always get a couple of volunteers to drive the revelers home, you know, because of the drinking. I don't see why we can't convince one of them to get you early. Let's see. Oh here's Matt." Her voice muffled as she spoke to someone in the background, and then a man came on the line.

"Hello, Matt Granger here."

Kaleena grinned at the deep, sexy tone. Not as hot as Cody's of course. "Hey, Matt Granger, can you give me a ride to the party? My name is—"

Cody snatched the phone from her. "She has a ride."

He stabbed the End button and tossed her phone onto the table. "Be ready to go at six-thirty, and don't expect to stay late."

She followed Cody as he stomped from the room, hands on her hips. "What was that about? You said you weren't going, so I made other arrangements."

"I'm taking you now, so drop it." He kept walking.

"Does it have to do with that guy? What was his name, Matt Granger?"

He whirled on her and grabbed her by the arms. She stared up into his eyes. "Kaleena, I said let it go."

"Okay, fine." He released her, and she rubbed the spot where he'd held her arms. "I hope you're not going to be a grump all night."

He eyed her hand. "Did I hurt you? I'm sorry. I never meant…"

"It's okay. I'm not hurt." She pointed a finger in his chest. "And you're not stopping my happy, Cody 'Scrooge' Everett. I'm going to have a good time."

* * * *

Kaleena wore over the knee black boots with a purple long-sleeved minidress that form-fitted to every curve. The V neckline plunged low enough to show off a little cleavage but not enough that her boobs would freeze. She curled her hair and styled it high on her head at the back with soft tendrils and bangs to accent her face. Silver diamond shaped earrings hung from her ears, and she matched those with bangles on one wrist. If she did say so herself, she looked hot. Her boots, sexy in design, had a low enough heel that she could dance the night away—or at least until grouchy Cody dragged her home.

She laughed at her reflection in the mirror and then left her room, ready on time. When she walked along the hall, Cody already stood at the end of it near the front door. He'd worn a black turtleneck shirt, material thick enough to keep him warm but not so overwhelming he'd burn in the barn. The dark slacks showed off his hard muscled legs, which she'd gotten plenty of chance to run her hands over when they had sex, but her gaze snagged on the growing tent at the front of his pants. Apparently, he liked her outfit.

Kaleena stopped and spun in a slow circle. She put a hand on her hip and stuck her ass out. "How do I look?"

His green eyes flashed in the hall lighting. "You know you look good."

"But I like to hear it." She came closer and rested her hands on his chest, smiling up at him. The big chest rose and fell with his rough breaths.

"You're beautiful and sexy."

"Thanks." She stretched to her toes and kissed his lips. "I'm ready."

They left for the party, Kaleena curling into Cody's

truck. As they made a U-turn, she spotted the lights on at the house where Cody said his brother lived. She wondered what they were up to and if Beau had a woman or a friend that helped him get off his butt and stop hating Christmas. She hadn't met Cody's brother except in passing last year, but he seemed like a good man, and he deserved better. They both did.

When they drew up to the place, Kaleena understood why Cody had called it a barn party. The building looked exactly like a barn, from the two extra wide doors at the front with slats of wood forming Xs decorating them to the walls made from more wood and the slanted roof over the top and the two wings on each side. A gigantic wreath with a red ribbon at the base hung from the upper wall. Barrels held evergreen plants at the entrance. When they drew close, she noticed the doors slid apart on a track rather than opening out like a regular barn. Music blared from the interior, someone playing a fiddle as well as other instruments.

Inside was wall-to-wall people, but Cody didn't lie about the expansive floor space. Strings of white lights had been strung along the rafter overhead. Wreaths adorned each post. On the walls hung sets of reins as if waiting for a horse and rider.

Kaleena leaned in to Cody. "Is there a bathroom here?"

"At the back." He nodded in the general direction, and

she spotted an opening that might lead to where she saw the left wing of the barn. On the other side, a long table had been pushed to the wall, and a punch bowl adorned the middle. Around it were cups and food. Kegs of beer sat on another table and coolers she assumed held bottles of beer.

"Welcome, welcome, and Merry Christmas!" An older woman in a Mrs. Claus costume strode up to them. She held out little stickers. "I'm Jen, your happy hostess for the evening. Hold onto these stickers because they correspond to the gifts we have from Santa. Now get on in here and enjoy the party."

Kaleena smiled and thanked her, but she didn't tell her she'd spoken with her on the phone. The fact that Cody had hung up on her, or rather the other man, was bad enough. She would just enjoy herself. "Come on, Cody. Let's dance. I feel the need to get my freak on."

He cast a glance in the direction of the live band, and she laughed taking his hand.

"Hey, it's a beat. Not really what I listen to, but I can move to just about anything."

He gave in, and she tugged him toward the middle of the floor. Kaleena snapped her fingers and wiggled her hips to the rhythm. She moved in close to Cody, teasing him, and then backed up. His heated gaze never left her body when she didn't want it to and locked on her eyes when she caught him there. The entire time, his movements were minimal at best. She laughed and turned her back to him to guide his hands to her hips.

"Move with me," she coached him.

Her ass brushed his thigh, sending a zing of desire coursing through her veins. He dipped his head low, bringing his mouth close to her ear. Kaleena felt like she could slip away until there was no one but the two of them, but she turned her head and took in the crowd. Through the throng of bodies, she spotted a man standing near the wall with a beer in his hand. On his head, he wore a Santa hat, but his clothes were no different in their casual yet sexy appeal than Cody's. The man focused on her, and when he caught her looking, he raised his bottle. She offered him a friendly smile and looked away.

A shout went up in the crowd, and a line formed around the tree farther back in the room. "Conga line?" Kaleena laughed. "What the hell. Let's join them."

Cody hung back. "I'm getting a beer."

She saw the tension around his mouth and eyes. He really didn't like this scene.

"Okay, mind if I do?"

"Enjoy." He walked away. She balled her hands into fists until her fingernails hurt the soft flesh, then ran over to join the others. If Cody wanted to be a bore, he could do it alone. Falling into line with everyone else, she *whooped* along with them. After that craziness, she didn't lack for partners, and Cody didn't return to her side. She caught a glimpse of him cornered by several women and frowned.

"We can't have that," someone said to her left. "A beautiful woman should not frown at a party."

She whirled to face the man she'd seen earlier. His blond hair and blue eyes would have been hot even without the broad shoulders, but there was also insincerity in his bearing. Still, she wasn't there to find a boyfriend, so he might be fun.

"Are you offering to help me enjoy myself?" Flirting came easy when it meant nothing.

"I will make it my duty." He put his hand out, and she took it. They whirled into a dance to the next song, and like she'd done with Cody, this man moved close to her. She retrieved her hand from his grasp and spun around as if it were all a part of her dance. He chuckled, and she knew he wasn't fooled. "Matt Granger. You are?"

She missed a step. So this was the guy that made Cody bring her to the party.

Matt raised his eyebrows. "Did my reputation precede me?"

"Um, no. I'm Kaleena. Kaleena Morgan. Good to meet you, Matt. Should I be worried about your reputation?"

He drew her closer with a hand at her waist. "Only if you mind me stealing your heart."

Full of ourselves, aren't we? "Oh, I think I'm good."

She tried getting space between them, but he didn't allow her to go far. Not that she didn't enjoy the strong hands and big build of a sexy man, but Matt seemed too confident, like she should fall at his feet and beg him to take her. *Not happening, pal.*

At the end of another song, Kaleena fanned herself. "It's getting pretty hot in here."

"Can I get you a beer?"

"I'm not really a beer person."

"Punch then?"

"Sure, thanks." She decided to follow him and see if she could get a napkin to wipe down her forehead. Stepping outside might not be a bad idea either. She watched him get her punch and took the offered cup. A sip of the oversweet but ice cold drink helped. Kaleena scanned the room for Cody.

"If you're looking for your date, he's over there." Matt pointed him out talking to yet another woman. From Kaleena's angle their bodies looked like they touched, and Cody didn't appear put off. *Bastard.*

"Oh, he's not my date. Come on. Let's dance." She dragged Matt onto the floor again, and he didn't seem to mind. When he drew her in close until her hips just brushed his upper thighs, she let him. While most people appeared to move in one spot, she and Matt shifted positions. If she didn't know any better, she would suspect him of dancing her nearer to Cody on purpose. When the cute little pixie hanging on Cody stood on her tiptoes to whisper something in his ear, Kaleena had had enough. "Mind if we get some air?"

"Sure." Matt led her through the throng, her hand in his. They found their coats and stepped out into the cold winter night. Kaleena hugged herself and shuffled from one foot to the other to generate some heat. Matt led her to an area at the side of the building where a wall blocked off most of the wind. "Better?" he asked.

She nodded, grateful to him. "Thanks."

He rubbed palms up and down her arms with brisk movements. "Why does that thanks sound like surprise? Did you assume I'm the kind of man who thinks only of myself?"

"I'm sorry. I shouldn't jump to conclusions. I don't know you, but I think you know Cody, right?"

He hesitated, but she held his attention. "Cody and I were rivals in school. Sometimes I got the girl. Sometimes he did. Simple as that."

"Hm."

"That answer it for you?" He reached up to touch a strand of her hair. She resisted ducking away. His answer explained why Cody didn't want Matt to take her to the party. Their old competition thing rose in him, so it wasn't really about her. Not that she wanted it to be. She'd made a mistake letting feelings get in the way of dealing with Cody. Then again, what had she expected coming here?

She liked him—*a lot*. What he did for her could not be measured in words or in deeds as far as she was concerned.

"Yes, that answers it." She started to pull away, but Matt stopped her with heavy hands on her shoulders.

"Are you having a good time?"

"Yes, inside I was. All the energy and lights and colors. Everybody is so excited." Her eyes widened, when she realized how insulting to him she'd just sounded. "I'm sorry. I didn't mean…"

"No, don't apologize. Maybe we can have a little more fun out here." He stepped forward, but she put her hand up to his chest.

"Really? You're sensing me wanting your kiss right now?"

He froze at her blunt statement, and Kaleena almost laughed.

"I admit I'm flattered. I like the attention just like any other woman would, but I'm not a fool either. I've dated guys like you who are just looking for your next lay."

"You don't know me as we—"

"I don't have to know you well." She crossed her arms over her chest. "So you weren't going to kiss me?"

"I think we got off on the wrong foot." He uncrossed her arms and kissed the fingers of one hand. She pulled to get away, but the pressure increased, just short of hurting her. Matt didn't know but he was about to get a knee to the balls. She wondered if she should warn him. No, let him find out when he lay in the snow curled up like a little boy. Just as it seemed earlier, his expression reflected that he knew what she thought. More than one woman must have damaged the jewels—or tried. "Tell me you weren't using me to make him jealous."

"I wasn't."

The obvious disbelief irritated her.

"Cody doesn't fall for that kind of thing. When a woman he's seeing tries to make him jealous, he just moves on. His philosophy is if she wants to be with another man, she can. No one woman is as important to him as his next conquest."

"Aren't you just talking about yourself?" Hurt welled up inside of her. She cursed herself for it because she and Cody were not a couple. "I have to go in. My toes are starting to freeze."

She began to move around him when he drew her into an embrace and locked his lips on hers long before she saw him coming. His tongue swept the inside of her mouth, and she cringed in disgust. Before she could raise her knee, Matt was wrenched away from her. She gasped finding Cody standing there. He jerked Matt up by the collar and planted a fist in his nose. Matt hit the ground, blood staining his lips, chin, and his coat.

"Cody!" She glared at him. He had a nerve coming out here acting like he had some kind of rights. For all he knew, she might have wanted Matt's touch. She gagged thinking of it, but Cody didn't need to know. "Why did you do that?"

"I thought you came to a Christmas party," Cody snapped.

She put her hands on her hips. "And what?"

"Shouldn't you be inside? They're passing out gifts."

She rolled her eyes at him and walked past. Matt was busy shaking his head and pinching his nose. She stepped over him and strode back to the barn with her head held high.

Once she entered the building, the festivities of the evening held less of an appeal, but she determined she would stick it out and let Cody stew. Only when she realized neither she nor he was making any enjoyable memories, she called it a night. At least her secret Santa had given her a cute bear ornament for the tree she intended to make Cody put up in the living room. In his truck, Kaleena removed her boots and rubbed her feet. She winced at the sore spots.

"If you want, I can rub them for you when we get home," Cody offered.

She stared at him. Hadn't he made a date or whatever to hook up with one of those women? Or did he tell her to hold off until his unwanted guest left? She chewed her lip thinking it over. "I wouldn't want to put you out."

The steering wheel squeaked under his hold. "I don't

Nobody's Lover

know why you're so angry at me. Matt has a sort of reputation with the women."

"And you don't?"

He grunted, never taking his eyes off the dark road. "Not like that."

"Please explain it because I'm not sure I understand." How could he think her anger had anything to do with him hitting that asshole?

"Nothing's ever been proven or even gone to court, but Matt doesn't take no for an answer. I have never forced a woman and never will."

Kaleena gasped. "Are you serious?"

"Yes, that's why I didn't want him to drive you. I knew he would try something. I thought it safe as long as you two danced."

So he *had* noticed.

"Then I lost sight of the two of you. I searched all over that damn place."

"I can take care of myself. Thanks. After all you were busy having fun of your own." She swore in silence, not meaning to reveal her jealousy.

Cody eyed her briefly but said nothing. Kaleena just kept herself from gritting her teeth. The man didn't give a freaking inch. He could deny it or say "yeah, so what." Then she could modify this hero image she had of him in her head, which begged the question of whether she felt only gratitude toward him and nothing else. Even her sexual attraction to the man might be no more than infatuation with his kindness last year.

Yeah, real funny, Kaleena. The man is hung, and he can get you screaming in a hot minute. That ain't kindness!

They strode into the house a short while later. She started to her room and stopped to look back at him. "Can you take me to get a tree tomorrow?"

He frowned. "Isn't it a little too late?"

"Please?"

He sighed. "Fine. Anything else?"

She smiled and walked over to him. Hands on his chest, she tipped her head back. "We should exchange gifts, and if you agree, I can do some shopping for you. Plus, you need to tell me what you want for Christmas dinner, so I can cook it."

"Kaleena..."

"I like when you say my name. It sounds funny but cute."

His brows went up. "I pronounce it just as you do."

"That's what you think."

His eyes narrowed on her lips. "You are a very dangerous woman, Kaleena Morgan. I'm a simple man, who lives an ordinary life here on my ranch. You—"

"I'm what?" She opened her eyes wide in an attempt at innocence. At the same time, she closed more of the space between them. "What is it? I know I'm not like the women here that you're used to."

"Definitely not!"

She wasn't sure how to take that, whether he complimented her or felt disgust that she'd even make the comparison. Cody had kept his hands firmly by his sides while she leaned into him, but now he brought them up to her waist. He gave her a small squeeze and then set her away.

"I'm trying to do the right thing by you," he muttered.

"Why?"

He growled and turned on his heel to stomp toward the kitchen. No matter how hard she tried, she didn't get the man. He never explained himself. Unless she missed her guess, he treated her better than he did the other women. None of them got to go home with him, but then again, she could be the flavor of the month—chocolate flavor. She had been in a terrible place last year, and he didn't get to sleep with her. Now he made up for the lost opportunity.

Kaleena went to her bedroom and stood at the dresser, staring into her reflection. "Stop being negative." She had a good figure, and she liked to think she was pretty. That didn't mean every man should or did want her, but Cody enjoyed the sex. If that was all he wanted, he wouldn't have put her away just now.

She jumped when he appeared in the mirror behind her. His footsteps never echoed in the hall. Peering down, she found he'd removed his boots and socks. Even his feet were sexy, neat and clean, big and strong with straight toes unaffected by wearing cowboy boots so often.

His hands roamed up her arms to her shoulders, and he massaged her neck, bringing a moan to her lips. "You want it?" he asked.

She met his gaze. "Yes."

Hadn't she just said he saw her differently than the rest because he didn't pursue sex? Now she didn't know what to think, but she refused to turn him down. She wanted him just as badly, and if his body was her weakness, she didn't mind being his. He pushed her coat over her shoulders and threw it aside. Then reached for the zipper at the back of her dress.

When she stepped out of her dress and removed her boots, she reached for his belt buckle, but Cody stopped her. "No, tonight I'm starting with you."

"But we…"

"I've been waiting to taste your pussy, and I'm going to right now. I hope you like being eaten, Kaleena." He dropped to his knees and dragged her panties over her hips. She shivered, capturing her bottom lip between her teeth. Just watching him down there had her pussy weeping.

"Of course, but I know this is new. I don't want you to do something you might not like."

He raised an eyebrow and helped her to step out of her

underwear. His hands skimmed her legs, and she was glad she'd shaved them. *"This* isn't new, baby." He kissed between her thighs, and she grasped the dresser to hold herself up. "Mm, you taste good. You knew that, didn't you?"

He didn't wait for an answer but ran his tongue over her clit and along her folds. She pulled away a little, gasping, but Cody drew her to him and used his thumbs to open his way to her cream. His tongue slid into her channel and wiggled, sending shockwaves of pleasure all over her body. Kaleena knotted her fingers in his hair and drew him forward. He laved her juices as they flowed, and she moaned his name.

"Yes, don't stop. So good. Make me come, Cody."

He closed his lips over her clit and sucked once, hard. She screamed. Her orgasm came so fast, she didn't know it was close. Cody stood up and pulled her to the bed. He shoved her down and dove between her legs, eating her come as it dribbled down her channel. Kaleena pinched her clit and rode her lover's face. She spread her legs as wide as they would go, and for a long time, Cody didn't stop. When the sensitivity of her little bud eased, he went after it once again.

"No, stop," she whimpered.

"Do you really want me to?" His eyes were twin pools of swirling green sea, and they pulled her in. She opened her mouth to speak, but he went back to teasing her button. She squirmed and raised her hips. Cody pressed them down, pinning her to the bed. She loved his strength and enjoyed giving over control. When he paused, she thought she would cry. "Tell me, Kaleena. Do you want me to stop?"

"N-no."

He blew on her wet sex, making her shiver. "I can't hear you."

She licked her lips and swallowed, trying to appear calmer than she was. Right now she belonged to him, her whole body his to toy with or to cherish. She didn't dare think about whether he began to capture her heart. That might mean more pain. Still looking away from his gaze seemed impossible.

"Talk to me," he insisted.

"I don't want you to stop. Not until I've come again and again. Then I want to please you. If that's okay."

"More than okay." He sat up and dragged his shirt over his head. Kaleena feasted her eyes on his hard chest and traced it down to his navel. She couldn't wait until he took off his pants so she could see what interested her the most about his amazing body. When he lowered the zipper and shoved the slacks over his hips, she panted. His cock, thick and long, jutted from his crotch toward her. She took hold of it and ran her palm up and down its length. Capturing the precome on her thumb, she smeared it around the head and dipped down lick it clean.

Nobody's Lover

"Baby, baby, no," he moaned. "Not yet. Damn, how can I resist those sweet lips wrapped around my cock? Just watching you drives me crazy. But no, I'm going to eat you again. I want you coming in my mouth and screaming my name."

"But..."

"Lie down, Kaleena." He pushed her pack and raised one of her thighs. When he brought his teeth down on her ass cheek, she let out a small squeak, but he licked the stinging skin. Then he planted hungry kisses all the way up and around to her pussy. She squirmed, wanting more but so sensitive. Each touch made her nerve endings sing, and another orgasm began to build. Cody moaned against her pussy lips and drove his tongue inside her. He pinched her clit between his lips and tugged. She came unhinged. Her core muscles contracted, and she climaxed hard. Scratching at the covers and thrashing her head side to side, she cried out until it ended. When she was done, she struggled to catch her breath.

"Oh my goodness," she said in a raspy tone. "I didn't mean to get that loud."

"Don't apologize. I wanted to please you, and I did." He touched her cheek. She turned her face into his palm and kissed it, closing her eyes. She didn't mean for the movement to appear so intimate, so loving, so she pulled back and ducked her head. Cody raised her chin. He touched his lips to hers, and she tasted her own essence there. When he drew away, their gazes locked, and she thought she saw something in the depths of his eyes that couldn't be true. He broke the connection first. "I want to get inside you."

"I get to suck your dick," she told him.

"You don't have to."

"I want it." She gave him a glare and grabbed for her prize. Leaning in, she stuck out her tongue and gave it a swipe. Cody's breath hissed between his teeth. She took the head into her mouth and sucked. His smooth, leathery skin turned her on, and she licked him from tip to base. She sucked at his ball sac, taking first one into her mouth, released it, and took in the other. Afterward, she worked her way up his shaft and fed it between her lips. She moaned, laving him all over. Loving his scent and the way he moaned, she gave a small nip to the sensitive skin and teased him by gently skimming her teeth over his cock.

Cody swore. "Suck it, baby. You're going to force me to come."

She paused. "That's exactly what I want."

She swallowed his cock and took it as deep as she could. The thick head touched the back of her throat, and she worked him in and out of her mouth. His shaft throbbed beneath every stroke, and she sucked harder. Cody chanted her name. He squeezed her shoulder and dragged her closer. He began moving his hips at an unhurried pace, driving his big cock in and out of her mouth. She moaned as she took it and didn't stop until he gave a sharp cry and come flooded her mouth. Kaleena swallowed while Cody groaned and held himself still. When he was empty, he pulled out and raised her up into his arms.

"You're amazing," he whispered, his mouth in her hair.

She held onto him, her eyes shut and rested her head on his shoulder. Emotions choked her so she couldn't speak. Cody opened her legs so she straddled him, and they sat that way for long silent moments.

"I'll take you tomorrow," he said.

She sat up. "What?"

"I'll take you to get the tree and whatever else you want."

She smiled. "Can we exchange gifts? You know you want to."

He chuckled. "Fine. We will exchange gifts, but I'm not saying I'm excited about it."

"You don't have to. I'll be bubbly enough for both of us." She leaned back and grabbed hold of his cock. "Now how soon can I get this hard enough for me to ride?"

Cody's eyes seemed to blaze, and his shaft twitched in her hand. He raised her off his lap and stood up. When he led her over to the chair in the corner, she followed along, not knowing what to expect but not caring either. Cody would make her feel good and bring her to another orgasm soon enough. She let him lead. When they reached the chair, he made her face it and bend across the arm. Resting her palms on the seat, she glanced over her shoulder. Cody stroked her ass cheeks and spread them.

"Do you know how beautiful your pussy is?" he asked.

Goose bumps broke out on her skin. "It is?"

"Yes, and I could look at it all day and night."

"That's because you're dirty, and your mind is always on sex."

"Are you complaining?"

She wiggled her hips. "No." He dropped to his knees and kissed her pussy. She moaned. When he stood and took his cock into his hand, she held him off. "Condom."

He swore, and she laughed. "I'll get one."

She ran out into the hall knowing where he kept the condoms in his room. When she found one, she hurried back toward her room but then returned to the living room. On the mantel over the fireplace, she'd left a Santa hat because she wasn't sure what she would do with it. She grabbed it and headed to her room.

"Will you be my Santa?" The sultry voice and posing naked seemed to do it for him. Cody's cock rose while he nodded. She sashayed over to him and plunked the hat on his head, handed him the condom, and then positioned herself over the arm of the chair, on her toes and ass in the air. "Fuck me, Santa."

Nobody's Lover

"How can I say no to that offer?"

After he put on the condom, he moved behind her. His gaze drank in the sight of her until goose bumps rose on her skin. She'd never felt so appreciated, so attractive. Instead of thrusting into her right away, he seemed to savor the moment, running his hands along her sides. He pulled her upright and kissed her shoulder before nuzzling her cheek.

"Cody?"

"Shh." He reached around her and turned her head toward him to kiss her lips. Their noses brushed, and Cody held her tight to him. "There's something about you."

"You said that before." She dared not read into it.

"Stay."

She gasped, not sure how to take that one word, but Cody didn't repeat it. He held her hips and thrust into her pussy. She moaned and pushed back to him. Gently, at an easy pace, he sank deep, until he filled her. They moved as one, a rhythm and pleasure that robbed her of the ability to analyze his desires.

"Take it all, Kaleena."

"Yes," she moaned.

"All of me."

She cried out when an orgasm began to build. Cody cupped her pussy, parting his fingers around his shaft as he continued to thrust into her. He picked up the pace and began slamming it home. The sensations drove her to the brink of climax, and she hovered there. She wriggled her hips and grabbed the back of Cody's thigh to drive him forward. The nails of her other hand scratched at the chair's fabric. She screamed his name.

"I need it. I need it!"

"Yes, baby, feel it," he demanded. "I want you to come with me."

"I don't know if I can."

He shifted their position just a little to draw her knee up on the chair arm. She angled her hips, and Cody didn't lose momentum. He plunged into her wetness, sending quakes to every corner of her being.

"You like that, Kaleena?"

"Yes!"

"Do you want me to pump harder?"

"Yes!"

Cody caught her clit between two fingers and played with it, tugging and massaging. His thick shaft disappeared up her channel at lightning speed, and even the slap of their bodies coming together took her higher. When the sensual waves began, she whimpered and dropped her chin to her chest.

"Mm, there it is," Cody murmured. "Now, let go. Give yourself to me, Kaleena. *Damn!*"

His release must have hit, because his voice went deeper, and he gave a powerful thrust and stayed buried inside of her. A harder pinch to her clit put Kaleena over the edge, and she came along with him. They panted together, her jaw slack and eyes closed. When she calmed down, Cody pulled out and lifted her in his arms. They moved to the bathroom for a hot shower together before falling into bed.

Chapter Seven

"This one. It's perfect," Kaleena exclaimed. She pointed out the tree she wanted, and Cody made the arrangements for its purchase. Pride didn't keep her from arguing with him when he said he'd pay for the tree and all the decorations. Her funds were limited, and she was just glad he agreed to do this. On top of that, she didn't think he appeared as grumpy about it as all the other times.

That morning they had awakened in each other's arms and made love before getting out of bed. Kaleena waited for Cody to explain what he meant by "stay," but he didn't broach the subject again, and she was too scared to find out he didn't mean what she thought. If he truly wanted her to live with him, then he needed to make it plain. But would she do it? As irrational as it sounded, she'd come to feel a long-term serious relationship for her was not in the cards, and giving in to it meant trouble. In her mind, she liked the idea of a man like Cody. In reality, it scared the crap out of her.

They hit store after store, even small gift shops where

Nobody's Lover

she discovered collectible ornaments. She chose cute little snowmen with felt scarves and real buttons for eyes, straw sticks that had been bent to spell the word *joy*, and a bulb that looked like Santa's belly with his red coat and black belt. Cody wandered over holding other small items.

"What about this one?" he suggested.

She took a look. "What is that?"

"A bison."

"You're kidding me. What's this other one? A bale of hay?" She was about to tell him to put them back and stopped herself. This was his Christmas, too, and she wanted him to enjoy every part. Maybe seeing the weird ornaments he chose would give him happiness years from then. She grinned. "What the heck, let's get them."

He smirked. "See, I can decorate even though I haven't done it since I was a kid."

She laughed. "Uh-huh, sure."

Cody hefted the tree into the bed of his truck, and Kaleena ran off to do more shopping. She wandered around stores looking for the perfect gift for Cody. A shop selling leather goods caught her eye, and she pushed open the door, a bell jingling overhead. The scent of real leather tickled her nose, and she looked around. The large journal with handmade paper drew her in an instant. Maybe Cody could do his ledgers or something for his business.

"Great choice, miss," the proprietor said walking up. "If you like we can even have it engraved with the

100

recipient's name."

She hesitated and glanced around. Did everyone in this town know Cody? Would it annoy him to have the people know she bought him such a gift? Then again, if he were that concerned, he would have tossed her out of his house. Everyone must know she was staying there.

"How soon can it be ready?" she asked.

"I can have it done by tomorrow afternoon."

"Awesome."

They headed to the register, and she wrote down the name she needed engraved on the front of the journal. The man peered at it, and his eyebrows rose. *So much for hoping he doesn't know Cody.*

He studied Kaleena, and she endured it for the moment. Of course, he had five seconds to move past who she was and finish the transaction. If he didn't, she would give him an earful.

"You know, I can probably do a drawing down the bottom right here, of the entryway to Twin Falls Ranch." He demonstrated on a piece of paper, flooring her with his talent.

"Yes! Do that, please."

The man laughed. "You got it. I think Cody will enjoy this gift from the special lady in his life. Don't you?"

She looked away. "I'm just a friend, but thanks so much. I'll come back tomorrow."

Kaleena made a few more purchases and headed back

to where Cody parked the truck. She opened the door, which he'd left unlocked and dumped her bags, not trusting them for the back. Cody must have dropped off a few things of his own, because she spotted a huge bag beside the tree. She started to reach in and be nosy, but a female voice calling out to Cody stopped her.

The little pixie from the night before posed not ten feet from where Kaleena stood. Kaleena glanced past her to see Cody walking along the street, hands in his pockets. He looked directly at the woman, and Kaleena's stomach muscles clenched.

"How about my offer, Cody? We can have a lot of fun." The sultry tone and beautiful face and figure had no doubt brought more than one man to his knees. Kaleena gritted her teeth and fought to keep her expression neutral. She had a feeling she failed miserably, but Cody hadn't looked in her direction yet.

When he drew close to the woman, Kaleena and the skank both gasped as he strode right by without a word. Kaleena froze when he stopped in front of her and removed her hand from the bag in the back of the truck. "Get out of there. You don't get to look yet."

She blinked at him. "Cody, did you hear—"

"Let's go, or are you not finished shopping?"

She licked her lips. "I'm done."

He opened the door for her, and she climbed inside. While Cody strode around to the other side, she searched for the woman. She hadn't moved but stood frozen to the spot, mouth hanging open. When she caught Kaleena staring, she scowled and pivoted on her heel to flounce away. Kaleena couldn't help feeling sorry for the woman. Cody didn't have to be so harsh, but then again, maybe at the party he'd told her no. None of them liked losing a man such as him.

He settled behind the steering wheel of the car and turned over the engine. She studied his strong hands, his firm jaw, and those amazing eyes. He wasn't wordy, and he kept his own business. She imagined he'd satisfied the sexual itch when the mood struck and bet he made it clear there would be no relationship. The funny thing was, he'd never said as much to her, not even a hint. *"Stay."*

The word tormented and delighted her at the same time. So much meaning in a single utterance, and in some ways, she wanted to remain in the dark about his intentions. This Christmas so far, spending it with him, was like a fairytale unfolding, and she had no illusions about the ending. While it lasted, she would have fun.

"Decorating and cooking when we get home," she announced. "And I bought more tins so we can package up goodies for your staff. We'll suck down too much eggnog, and I will put the turkey in the fridge."

Cody nodded, a slight smile on his face. She tried to remember if he ever smiled like that without her having to push him. Her heart beat faster in her chest, and moisture built in her eyes. When they got home, Cody brought the tree in along with the bags. Kaleena headed for the kitchen. She settled on dinner and put the turkey in the fridge before returning to the living room to help with the tree. Cody stood at her side taking her orders like a soldier. She had to bite back a laugh time and again. He really was sweet in his way.

"What was your life like as a child?" she asked. "Did y'all decorate?"

He seemed to hesitate. "We did, every year. My mom went all out like you're doing. That's why it was difficult after…"

"I'm sorry." She toyed with one of the figurines for the mantel. "Sometimes the girls at school talked about shopping with their mothers, and I'd get so jealous, but Uncle Cornell made up for it when he could. It wasn't the same, but I knew he loved me. Besides, how can you miss something you never had, right?"

"You can, and you do." Cody pulled her close and kissed her. Kaleena settled in his embrace, breathing in his familiar scent. She wondered how he could become so much a part of her so quickly. Last year they'd formed a bond, she realized, and her leaving hadn't broken it. That's why she could come back without notice, and he let her in. Did he understand it?

"Why were you rude to that woman? You could have told her you're not interested."

Cody released her and turned her toward the tree. "Let's finish this. I'm starving."

She grunted. "You're so stubborn."

He placed the bison on a branch of the tree. She resisted moving the bulky weird thing to a spot in the back. When they were done, the tree looked amazing. Kaleena took the time to *ooh* and *ahh* over it, and to her surprise, Cody disappeared from the room only to return with a camera and tripod. They took pictures in front of the tree and the fireplace, and Kaleena turned on Christmas tunes.

"I have something for you I want to give you early," Cody said.

She thrilled that he got into the mood of the season. "Really? What is it?"

He left the room once again and returned with the big bag she'd seen in the truck.

"I have wrapping paper if you want to wrap it first," she suggested.

"We'll use it right away. There's no point."

She rolled her eyes. "Men." Kaleena opened the bag to find a huge sled, and she gaped. "Wow! What am I going to do with this?"

"You're going to ride it—with me. You wanted to know what my brother and I did as kids? This is it. You and I are going to find a hill and ride this down it."

"Um, yeah, don't put me down for that." She turned to

run away, but he caught her around the waist and hauled her to his chest."

"Don't be chicken."

She laughed, the first hardy, deep laugh that went all the way down to the places that were still tender and painful. "Okay, but if I bust my ass, it's your fault!"

They found a hill with no problem, and being Wyoming, they had plenty of snow. The sled's build didn't give her much confidence with just a few wooden slats to sit on and a sort of crossbow look to it at the front where they would brace their feet. A rope was the only guidance that Kaleena could see.

"I'm not sure about this," she said in doubt.

Cody rubbed her back. "Don't worry. It will be fun."

"Says you. I suddenly feel old."

He kissed her lips and encouraged her to sit down in the front, while he positioned himself in back. With his arms around her waist, he scooted in very close, and the sense of safety that came over her took her breath away. This was Cody, the man who had stuck by her side during the worst time.

"Hey," he whispered in her ear.

"Hm?" She settled into his chest and nuzzled her face into the warmth of his against the wind. Despite trusting him, she hoped this little indulgence wouldn't last long. She did it for him and hoped the experience would be everything he remembered and more.

"Kaleena, look at me."

She opened her eyes and raised her head to meet his gaze.

"I walked by her because I don't want her or any other woman here. I have a past. That's been obvious from the beginning. I realize that, but I don't want you to think that's still me. It's not. After I met you..."

She shivered, and hung on his every word. He narrowed his eyes and then kissed her again.

"Come on. Let's go," he said. Before she could register that he cut off the conversation, they whisked down the hill with Cody holding the rope in front of her. Kaleena screamed, squeezing his knees at her sides. At first fear gripped her, and then fun kicked in. She *whooped* in delight and raised her hands in the air. Cody's grip tightened. When they reached the bottom, somehow they tumbled into the snow. "Kaleena!"

She lay flat on her face, the snow cold and biting against her skin. Cody jerked her up and into his arms. "Kaleena, are you okay? Baby, talk to me!"

She laughed. "If you shut up I will. I'm fine. That was incredible. Let's go again."

He frowned. "You're cold. We should—"

"Race you to the top!" She took off running, although gravity weighed her legs. Cody caught her and held her hand. For almost an hour, they rode down the hill and climbed back up. Kaleena had never had so much fun. On the way back to the truck, she pelted Cody with snowballs, and he chased her, capturing her with ease.

"You're going to pay for that, woman," he growled suggestively in her ear.

She squirmed, not even trying to get out of his hold. "I bet I will, but I'm not complaining. Whatever you want to do to punish me is fine with me."

The expression following Cody's shock had her laughing again, and he concentrated on getting them home.

Over the next day, Kaleena wrapped gifts and cooked. The house filled with the scent of roasted turkey, sweet potatoes, green beans, baked macaroni and cheese, and homemade biscuits. She added a chocolate cake and a pumpkin pie to the dessert menu. The fact that Cody stayed beside her, helping to prepare anything she asked him to when he wasn't taking care of his animals, warmed her heart beyond belief. She saw the contentment on his face more often than the sadness deep in his eyes.

"You know we can never eat all of this, don't you?" he asked in the midst of the process.

"You can have it all week and forget about that processed junk for a while."

He fell silent, and she wondered what was on his mind. "We're invited to my brother's place for dinner tomorrow. Apparently, he has met someone."

She stopped mid-stir with the gravy. "He has? And

they're having Christmas dinner?"

"So he tells me."

Kaleena studied Cody's face. He might appear nonchalant, but curiosity peeked through. She smiled. Miracles never ceased. The same time she had been working to make the holiday a happy time for her and Cody, another woman worked to help Beau. So much joy bubbled up inside, she felt like she'd burst. Tears spilled onto her cheeks, and she turned her back to Cody so he wouldn't see.

"That's cool." Hopefully, he didn't hear the emotion in her tone. "We can have a little something here and open presents, and then go there."

"Hm," he agreed and laid down the knife he'd been using the chop tomatoes. He wiped his hands on a dishtowel. "I have to take care of something. I'll be back later."

"Cody, there's so much more to do."

"I'll be back."

He disappeared, leaving her alone, and she sighed. Maybe all of this was too much for him, and he didn't want to change. She thought about what he'd said out on the hill when they went sledding. He wanted no other woman except her, but did he mean no other one while she visited? Something told her Cody wouldn't be the type of man to cheat. If he wanted another woman, he'd break ties with the first. So his "devotion" to her while

Nobody's Lover

they were together for Christmas wasn't shocking. That didn't mean he loved her either. She grunted in annoyance, wishing she knew once and for all what he felt.

And what do you feel, Kaleena?

She mulled it over for the next hour and a half, but her mind refused to come to a firm conclusion. The fact of the matter was, she feared deciding once and for all that she loved him. If she admitted it, even in her own head, she opened herself to more pain, which would defeat the purpose of her being there.

"No, I'm going to stay the course, see this through, and that's all. Then we'll have something great to look back on. Period. End of story!"

"You're muttering to yourself." Cody appeared in the kitchen doorway, and she jumped. Excitement brewed in his eyes, and his obvious attempt to hide it didn't fool her.

She glared at him. "Where did you go? I need some more help."

"You'll find out."

They completed all the cooking and preparation for Christmas day. Kaleena brought out several gifts wrapped in shimmery paper and placed them under the tree. She fixed Cody and herself a plate of sandwiches, and they enjoyed a glass of wine to round out the day. She curled up on Cody's lap, and they sat in comfortable silence watching the crackling fire.

Chapter Eight

Christmas Day, Kaleena woke with expectation and excitement in her heart. She crawled out of bed trying not to wake Cody and showered and brushed her teeth in the bathroom. Once she reached the kitchen, she brewed coffee and started on breakfast for the two of them and brought it to the living room. She set the tray down and dropped to her knees to sort through the gifts. A few were from her to Uncle Cordell, and two were from her for Cody. When she spotted a couple for her from her lover, she grinned and picked up the nearest box to shake with her ear close to the package.

"How old are you?" he asked from the doorway.

She let out a small squeak. "Don't scare me like that."

"Stop being nosy," he quipped.

"I wasn't being nosy."

"What do you call it?"

She rolled her eyes at him and put the box back.

Cody took a seat in the chair farthest from the tree and held out his arms. "Come here, baby."

Kaleena didn't have to be asked twice. She rushed

across the room and climbed onto his lap, feeling like the child he accused her of being when he wrapped her in his warm embrace. He raised her chin, grasping with a firm hold, and slanted his mouth over hers. She moaned, accepting his tongue as it slid between her parted lips. For long moments, they kissed, and when Cody raised his head, Kaleena was drunk off his loving. She wanted to stay just where she was and never let the outside world interfere or come between them. *Reality will come soon enough, but for now...*

"Let me get the tray before our food gets cold."

He released her, and she brought the tray closer. Cody pulled her on his lap, and they shared a plate of sausage and waffles, drizzled with blueberry syrup. "Mm," Cody moaned. "You're going to make me fat with all this food."

"Please, your body is hard as ever."

He smiled. "I'm hard in certain places." He demonstrated by moving under her. She didn't mistake the erection pressing against her ass, and an answering pulse passed through her pussy.

"Get your mind out of the gutter." She smacked his arm, and he leaned in and licked a bit of syrup from her lip. Kaleena trembled with desire.

"If you don't quit it, we're going to be back in the bedroom."

Cody slid his hand between her legs and gave her pussy a squeeze. She tried not to ride his palm like the slut she was. "I don't mind," he teased.

"Well I do. I want to open gifts and see what you got me."

"Fine. Go get some presents, but come back over here. I want you on my lap all day."

"Why do I feel like you're not talking about me just sitting there?" She studied him over her shoulder.

"No idea."

Kaleena laughed and hurried to grab a few presents. She returned to his lap as instructed and handed him the gifts she'd gotten for him. "Open these first please."

Cody tore into the paper with no reverence whatsoever for its beauty. He tossed the remains on the floor and pulled the box open. Her heart sang when he burst out laughing full force, the mirth so filled with genuine happiness.

"A cookbook?" he asked.

She nodded. "Yes, because I don't want you to keep eating that processed stuff. It's not healthy, and no one can live off of eggs. At least not the way you make them."

"Haha, funny." He tweaked her nose, and then his eyes softened. "Thanks. This shows you put in a lot of thought for me, and you can't imagine what that means, Kaleena."

She ducked her head and lowered her lashes, not wanting him to see just how much she thought of him. "There's another one."

Nobody's Lover

He opened her second gift and discovered the journal. His gasp and eyes wide with awe was all she needed to know she'd made a good choice there too.

"Kaleena."

"I hope you like it." She knotted her fingers in the sweat pants he wore.

Cody pulled her hand to his mouth and kissed it. "I can't believe you. I knew last year, but I can't believe…" He paused, his eyes shut, and she got to enjoy the way his dark lashes lay against pale cheeks. So cute. His babies would be adorable if he had any one day. Longing stirred inside her, but she pushed the emotions down. Her stay here was coming to an end.

"Cody?"

He studied the workmanship of the engraving and ran his fingers over it. "This is the Twin Falls Ranch entryway, and you've had my name carved into it."

"I thought maybe you could use it for your business. I hope you like it."

"I love it and you."

Kaleena froze. "W-what?"

Cody stood and put her aside to get more gifts from beneath the tree. He passed a couple to her, and she ripped into them the same way he did, but with trembling hands. Her mind raced. She told herself she'd heard wrong or that he made a mistake. In the emotional moment, he couldn't have meant to say he loved her.

She exclaimed over the beautiful dress he had bought her in sparkling silver. The hip hugging ensemble reached to mid-thigh, and the design on the back was little more than two strips of material crossing from butt to shoulders. Her lover had added matching strappy heels.

"Wow, this is amazing, and it's my size. I love it. Thank you, Cody."

"That's not all."

She looked around. "I don't see anything else."

"Stay right here." He left the room and returned a short while later. Kaleena stared at the tiny box in his fist, her chest aching. Cody lifted her from the chair and sat her onto his lap. "Kaleena, I—"

"Cody, you shouldn't...um..."

"Shh." He put a finger to her lips. "Let me do this. Just listen. *Please.*"

She nodded. Any second now she would pass out.

Cody drew in a breath and let it out. He held both her hands in his, big hands that engulfed hers and made her feel tiny yet safe. He stroked her skin with a thumb, sending zings of desire through her body, and after a long pause, he spoke.

"Kaleena, I never thought I'd meet a woman like you. Hell, I didn't think she existed. I didn't know what or if I looked for someone. If you asked me, I would have said no. I was content with my life. Then one day you walked in, and I fell before I knew what was happening."

Nobody's Lover

Her eyes widened, and she tugged her hands to free them. Cody let go, and she folded them in her lap. He didn't need to see how they shook.

He pulled the string on the small box wrapped with red paper since she made no move to take it from him. "I thought I'd never see you again, yet you showed up out of nowhere a week before Christmas. Just that one act changed this holiday for me. You didn't leave it there. You made it fun, and I promise you I will never forget this as long as I live."

Tears filled her eyes and ran down her cheeks. "I'm so glad. I wanted you to be happy."

"I *am* happy, Kaleena—with you. *Because* of you." When he presented her with the ring, holding it up until light from the fire reflected off the massive diamond, panic set in. He picked up her left hand, but she curled her fingers into her palm. "Baby, I love you, and I want you to be my wife."

Kaleena almost hit the floor scrambling off his lap. She backed away from him, her head spinning. "Oh no, Cody. I'm so sorry. You're the most wonderful man in the world, but I can't. I just can't. To say yes, around this time? I can't do it. I have to go. I need to get back home."

She spun on her heel ready to run out the door, her thoughts rolling over top each other, her vision blurred with tears. The sob she heard she was pretty sure came from her, and all she could think was Cody deserved better. Maybe she'd been a fool to assume the brokenness between the two of them would mend with a few scattered experiences of fun over the Christmas holiday. She should have thought more of him and what he felt, not her own selfish notions.

Kaleena made it to the hall before Cody caught her wrist and whipped her around to face him. His hold on her might be gentle, but no amount of wriggling freed her. He drew her closer, and she trembled at the warmth radiating off his body. Even his natural male scent teased her, along with the sensation of his chest brushing her nipples through her nightie. She raised her hands and tangled fingers in his T-shirt, not knowing if she wanted to push him away or pull him nearer.

"I'm sorry," he whispered, and she figured he took back the offer. "I can't let you go."

She blinked up at him. "What?"

"I loved you last year, Kaleena. Somehow during those weeks I looked after you, I fell in love, but that wasn't the time to make declarations after all you'd been through. I was forced to watch you walk away, knowing I would never see you again. That day was the hardest I've ever lived through, apart from when I first found out about my parents. I let you go back then because it was the right thing to do, but that can't happen again." He drew her tighter to his chest, and rested his cheek on the top of her head. "I can't go through this again. I can't have you walk away from me another Christmas. I love you. If you can't marry me, I understand. But please, baby... *Please* stay."

"Yes."

Cody picked her up and thumped her on the hall table. He drew her chin up with both hands at her jaw and leaned in to kiss her lips. Kaleena moaned beneath the onslaught of his tongue and the way he parted her legs to push between them. He left her mouth to explore her cheeks, to kiss her eyes and her temples. When he returned to her lips, he dropped his hands to the front of his sweatpants and dragged them low. With a flick of a finger, he shoved her panties aside at the crotch and filled her with his cock. Kaleena cried out his name. Her wetness allowed him easy entry, but her inner walls clenched his shaft, and she hooked her legs around his waist. Cody thrust deep inside of her, drew back only a few inches, and then pounded deeper.

He raised her legs higher and ignored how the table banged the wall each time he rammed his dick into her pussy. Kaleena gripped his shoulders and angled back to take all of him. She rained kisses along his throat and tasted the salty skin on his shoulder. Sucking and licking, she loved on him, hoping for the evidence of how much she loved this man to show up for the entire world to see. He'd chosen her, when she was broken and afraid—he'd made her special to him.

"You're going to make me come, Cody," she whimpered.

"That's the plan," he growled.

He pulled out and yanked her to her feet. With a twist, he had her facing the table. Once again, he ripped her panties aside and thrust into her heat. She arched her back and went up to her toes, doing her best to accommodate his thickness.

Cody's hunger and his rough treatment had her legs hanging into the table. He tried bracing them both with a palm on the wall, but he didn't slow his pace. She pushed into his drive and met him grind for grind. Their bodies knocked together so hard until she couldn't take it anymore. She had to let go. Her orgasm exploded, and she lost the ability to hold herself up. When she collapsed, Cody caught her. He held on and pumped nonstop until he found his own release.

At last, he pulled out, and she drew away from the table. The fronts of her thighs were red despite her brown skin. Cody dropped to his knees. "Oh damn, baby, I'm so sorry. Please forgive me." He kissed her thighs and stroked the tender skin. "I'm an idiot. You agree to stay with me, and I go and hurt you."

"It's okay." She touched his hair, tangling her fingers in the silky locks. "You really should get up from there though because you're getting me hot all over again."

Cody jumped to his feet and took her hand. "Come on. Let me do this right."

They headed upstairs to his room, and Cody relieved

her of her clothing before taking off his own. He stood in front of her and guided her hands to his chest. Kaleena luxuriated in the feel of his hard body, the rapid heartbeat beneath her palms. She stared into his eyes and saw the love she never thought she'd see or want to see in another man other than the fiancé she lost. Cody wasn't like Jeff had been, but he didn't need to be. Cody's attentiveness, his sweetness, and his strength made him the man she loved now.

"I thought I could never be with anyone else," she murmured. "Not because I didn't want to. My heart ached to love again and be loved. I just thought it wasn't meant to be, that nobody would care. As hard as I strove to heal, I doubted my ability. You were there from day one. You helped me stand up and live. I love you so much, Cody. I'll admit I'm scared about this, but like you, I can't see myself leaving. Even with the risk—"

"Shh, my love." He touched her cheek when she started to cry and thumbed the moisture away. "There's no risk, except to be cherished by me."

He raised her into his arms and laid her gently on the bed. When he followed her down, Kaleena spread her legs to allow him to settle between them. She moaned as his cock sank into her heat. Connected physically, they lay unmoving. Kaleena mentally opened herself to Cody, as tough as it was. She trusted him, and even while an ache of fear started in her belly, she stayed open. The torment and pain of her loss hadn't robbed her of the ability to be with another. Instead, she realized, it sealed her fate toward finding the kind of completion she'd known before. The miracle came with Cody—her rescuer, her friend, her lover. Fear would not keep her from holding onto him now and forever.

As Cody began pumping with slow, deliberate movements, she raised her knees and locked her heels behind him. Their fingers intertwined at their sides, they moved in perfect unison. Kaleena arched into him and concentrated on the sensations his amazing body elicited. She lifted her legs higher and felt the bump of his ball sac against her anus. Pleasure exploded on a new level, and she gasped when her pussy walls compressed around her lover's shaft. An orgasm began to expand outward from her core. She shuddered from head to toe. Between gasps of ecstasy mingled with a spasm of fear, she managed, "Cody, I will. I *will* marry you."

The End

At Last

DAHLIA ROSE

Chapter One

Beau Everett looked at the horse standing on the other side of the corral. He'd bought the stallion for breeding, and because he was just so damn beautiful. His coat was like black ink and shined like onyx. His lines showed perfect breeding and muscle tone, and Beau knew the name Midnight Ink was apt. But the stallion was stubborn, and now they were in the middle of a stare down. Even in winter he decided to work the horse. Wyoming was known for snowstorms as late as May. That was many months to wait, and the stubbornness set in. Midnight needed to be broken.

Beau puffed out a breath and watched it mist in the cold. Today wasn't bad, but he would prefer to take a horse and head to the hot springs in the mountain instead. Twin Falls ranch sat on a prime piece of property. The backdrop was Cloud Peak Mountain, and hot springs sat on their property. His father built the business from a small two-bedroom house to what it was now. After his parents died, he and his twin brother Cody took over the work and grew it exponentially since then. Cody managed

At Last

the cattle, and Beau always loved the horses. Except for right now with the battle of wills he had going with Midnight that had taken center stage for the past few weeks. He'd been working with the horse for weeks, and each day it was the same routine. Midnight refused to take the bit or be saddled.

"Staring him down working for you?" His brother's voice came from behind him and startled Beau. He was so intent on the horse that he didn't hear the boots crunching in the snow as Cody walked up.

"We're coming to a mental accord." Beau looked at his brother and grinned. It was like looking into a mirror except Beau ran his hand over the scar that was in the hairline over his right temple. At ten years old he thought he was a dare devil and tried to jump from the coral to the back of a horse . . . He missed.

"It seems he may be winning," Cody teased.

"I'm giving him the illusion of victory," Beau replied easily. "I saw your old friend drive up." A year ago, Cody spent a couple weeks helping a woman get over the loss of her fiancé. Beau saw her get out of the car at Cody's house a few days earlier. He also saw the look on his brother's face and the flush on his neck. There was more there than what his twin was saying.

"She just wanted to say hi," Cody answered.

"Uh-huh." Beau snorted. "Christmas lights in the window?"

Cody cleared his throat. "She likes the holiday."

"Apparently." Beau grinned. "Seriously, bro, I'm glad you seem to be taking that bull by the horns. You need someone in your life. I'm your big brother. I have to watch out for you."

This time Cody laughed. "By five minutes. That doesn't mean a thing."

"So you say, but I am more world savvy." Beau grinned.

"This year is sixteen years," Cody said suddenly.

Beau sighed. "I know. Didn't seem like that long since we lost them. I'll get flowers on Christmas day and take them to the graveyard."

"I'll be there. One more week till Christmas," Cody said. "Do you think they wanted this for us? The place looks like a sterile hospital on the holiday. Remember how Mom used to do it up? The house smelled like ham, bread and pies, and she even decorated the bunk house for the ranch hands."

Beau closed his eyes and remembered it easily. If he concentrated hard enough, he could swear he smelled her baking. Losing his parents still cut deep. Having them die on Christmas day made it even worse. He didn't know if they'd want this for him, but there was nothing about the holiday that brought him joy anymore.

"I hope Kaleena can help you enjoy it," Beau teased.

"You're a fine one to talk. By the way I went into

town this morning, and Natasha said hi," Cody said and punched Beau in the shoulder. "Bam, you should see your face."

His brother meant the hottest woman in Huntsford as far as Beau was concerned. They knew each other since high school, and she was always his unicorn. She moved to New York to be a photographer and then moved five years ago and bought Razzlez Bar and Grill." Upstairs she ran a studio taking pictures of babies and the residents of the town. Plus she worked at the small gazette taking pictures for the newspaper. She was a whirlwind packed into a pint size body being a mere five feet three inches to his six feet two. But when she entered a room, she dominated it. Her skin looked like it shimmered in the summer and was warm as hot chocolate in the winter. Big wide almond eyes would make any man fight a war for one look in their direction, and her full lips could curve in a smile or cuss like a sailor. *Perfect woman.*

"Earth to Beau, you're beginning to drool." Cody's voice held humor.

"Bite me sideways, Cody," Beau replied. "Go tend your cattle and let me work on this demon horse."

"Heading to Razzlez tonight?" Cody called over his shoulder as he walked away.

"Probably, the Friday night sunrise shooters are cool," Beau answered.

"That's all, huh?"

"Shut up, Cody," Beau yelled, and the response he got was a snowball in the back.

His brother's laughter faded away, and Beau faced Midnight again. Even though he needed to focus, Natasha's face came to mind, and a small smile crossed his face. Ok so maybe he was into her more than he let on. It could be the middle of summer and he'd want to kiss her senseless. The holidays brought up feelings that couldn't be trusted, especially with the loss of his parents and the feeling of loneliness that came with it. Beau didn't even want to think of Christmas, the cheer, and all the other stuff that came with it. He knew he sounded like a Scrooge, but it didn't matter. He was going to keep his head low until the New Year came in.

"Ok, Midnight, let's dance," Beau murmured and moved toward the horse. With slow, careful ease, he began trying to tame the willful animal once more, knowing full well that the next day he might have to start all over again.

* * * *

Rocking around the Christmas tree in a Christmas party hop. The music was up loud and holiday cheer in the air. Natasha Quinlan looked around the bar and smiled. This was her baby, and everyone seemed to be having fun. The dinner crowd had moved out and as per

At Last

Razzlez's way, the night was for couples, dancing, and fun. The pool tables were in use and the dartboards along the back wall. The Christmas tree in the corner had envelopes pinned to the branches, and she hoped it would be packed before the end of the night. Her patrons were pinning tips to it for the children's home in Huntsford. Natasha moved the little fuzzy ball of her elf hat back and scanned the room. The one person she wanted to see wasn't there, and she felt disappointment well up inside her. *Stop acting like a lovesick puppy*, she told herself. But it wasn't such an easy task to do. She left the town wanting to wrap her legs around Beau Everett and came back to find the feelings didn't change. The man was built like a linebacker in a cowboy hat. She had it bad for the part owner of Twin Falls Ranch.

The door opened, and a gust of wind brought in some of the snow flurries from outside. Beau walked in, and she swallowed a shot of vodka. It made her eyes water, and Natasha cussed in her head. He looked edible in the pair of blue jeans that hung just right on his hips. He wore a black long sleeve shirt tucked at his waist and tight across those big biceps and broad shoulders. His beat up cowboy hat made him look sexier than ever, and when he took it off, he ran his hand through his short hair as he looked around. Natasha had already averaged he was probably around forty-two inches from shoulder to shoulder. She wasn't the only one looking that's for sure, but when his blue green gaze landed on her, Natasha felt her heart beat a little faster. Especially when he walked over and sat his hat on the bar before sliding himself onto the stool.

"Evening, Ms. Natasha, you look festive as ever," Beau drawled.

"I could say the same for you, but I don't see mistletoe on that hat. I might have been tempted to kiss you under it," she said. "What are you drinking? Let me guess. A whiskey sour and a sunrise shooter."

"You know me so well. I may start to think you've got a vested interest in my happiness," Beau said.

"Stick around, you might find out," Natasha teased. She slid his drinks in front of him. "Enjoy." She felt his eyes on her as she moved down the bar.

The rest of the night got busier, and she didn't really have time to talk to him one on one. He left the bar and was playing darts with Carter Moore from the hardware store. *Shots n' darts, nothing good can come of it*, she mused. She left them alone. They were grown men letting off steam in a good way. Her wait staff was making good tips, and the crowd was a good one.

She changed the music, and the dancing started up just as she walked around the bar to serve some drinks to a group sitting in a booth. On her way back with an empty tray, she was caught around the waist and spun into a strong embrace. It was Beau who had the goofy look of having one too many. But when he pulled her close, her ass was pressed into the crook of his hips, and they began a slow roll. Her blood pressure went up a few notches.

"I've always wanted to have you in my arms like this," he said into her ear, and Natasha shivered.

She knew he was tipsy, that she should move, but for a second she reveled in the feeling before pushing away. "Ok, cowboy, you need to sit down before you fall down."

She led him over to a bar stool, and he sat on it heavily. She hated this time of year for him. He always overindulged for one day, and then he wouldn't be seen until the New Year. Everyone knew how Beau and Cody's parents died. The entire town had turned out for their funeral. Sixteen years later, it was still tearing the Everett boys up. That was how close of a family there were.

Natasha rang the bell and shouted. "Last call for alcohol!"

"I'll have a..." Beau began.

"Not you, Beau Everett. You get coffee, and then I'm driving you home when we close up," Natasha said sternly and pushed a cup in front of him. "You sit right there."

"Yes, ma'am, yes ma'am," he said and took a sip.

In about an hour the bar was clearing out and clean up began. The register was counted, wait staff pocketed their tips, and she ushered them out the door. In that time the snow fell harder. The heavy, thick flakes like soap bubbles hit the ground and stayed. There was no way she was going to risk driving to Twin Falls in this weather, and he certainly wasn't going to. She'd have to bunk him in her guest bedroom in her third floor apartment.

"I should get going," he said and got up from the stool.

"Take your ass upstairs, Beau. I'm going to call Cody and let him know you're not at your place, so he doesn't worry," Natasha said in the strictest voice possible.

"Aw, Tasha, you care about me." Beau pulled her into his arms. Her face was buried again his hard chest, and she could hardly breathe.

Natasha extricated herself and glared at him. "Yeah, I care. Now up the stairs."

When she bought the building, she had renovations done to put an extra set of stairs on the inside. The winter was fierce in Wyoming, and walking out into blizzard conditions to go to her home was not something she looked forward to. She made sure the doors were locked and turned lights off as she went upstairs behind Beau. In her fantasies this was when clothes came off and he whispered how much he loved her. Right now he could hardly find the laces of his boots if she wanted him to. Sometimes life was a fickle bitch.

In her apartment she directed him to her spare bedroom and sat him on the bed. He was docile as she

At Last

took his boots off and then his shirt before pushing him back in the bed.

"I've dreamt of you doing that," he said, and a sleepy grin crossed his face.

"Same here, but right now you're too snookered to appreciate me," she said gently.

"I'm going to kiss you senseless one of these days," he murmured.

She got his feet under the covers and pulled them up to his chest before she leaned over impulsively and kissed his forehead. "I look forward to it, but till then you get some sleep, stud."

He sighed and closed his eyes, and she watched him for a few minutes before turning the lights out and going down the hall to her own bedroom. Tomorrow he'd wake up and apologize for being drunk. Then they would go back to the way it was before, mild flirtation and casual friendship. Natasha got ready for bed and slipped between the covers. Before she closed her eyes, she wished things would change.

* * * *

The smell of bacon in the skillet woke her up, and she turned over to see it was only seven am. *Jeez, freaking cowboys and being up at the crack of dawn.* Natasha moaned and rolled over trying to bury her head under the

134

pillows. She was almost back to sleep when the whistling started, and she rolled out of bed with murder on her mind. She stood in the hallway to her living room area and looked across the wide expanse to her open kitchen. When she bought the building, she had the contractor take out the wall that separated the kitchen from the living room and use only a kitchen block as separation. Beau must've felt her glare because he looked up with a grin. Damn he even looked good early in the morning with his hair damp from the shower.

"Hey, I was going to wake you after the eggs were done," Beau said. "I took a shower and used your mouthwash."

"It's the ass crack of dawn."

"Seven am," he replied.

"Like I said the ass crack of dawn," she muttered. "Be quiet. I'm going back to bed."

"Not a morning person, are you?" Beau chuckled, and she sent him a dark glare. "Ok how about I put your breakfast in the oven, eat, and get out so you can sleep?"

"I'd cheer but I'm to sleepy," Natasha answered. She would regret her crabbiness when she woke up later, but right now, this was her with only four hours sleep.

Beau took the skillet off the stove and walked over to her. He wrapped his arms around her and pulled her into a big hug that lifted her off her feet. Natasha almost signed in pleasure.

At Last

"Thanks for crashing me out in your guest room," he said.

"You're welcome, and it was no big deal." She pushed her messy hair out of her face.

"I hope it was a big deal, and you don't let anyone sleep up here," he murmured. "I'd like to think I was special."

"You are, I mean… no one else has slept up here," Natasha stammered and cursed the effect he had on her.

"Let me make you dinner tonight at Twin Falls and a thank you for taking care of me," Beau said.

Natasha shook her head. "You don't have to do that."

"What if I want to do it?" he said. "Come on out and have dinner with me. You'll save me from another night of paperwork, bad TV, and an early bedtime. I make a mean steak on the grill."

"It's winter," she pointed out.

'Yeah but I can still grill. Come out and see my set up." Beau winked at her. She didn't even complain that he was still holding her. Now as he looked down at her, he rocked her back and forth. The sensation was quite pleasurable. "I'll make chocolate killer cake."

"Sounds deadly." She smiled.

"Extremely. I will have to make sure you don't curl up on my rug and purr like a kitten," Beau teased. "Hmm maybe I do want that. Say you'll come, Tasha."

He was the only one who ever called her that, and

dinner at his house had many implications. How could she refuse something she had hoped would happen for half her life?

"Ok, I'll leave Deena in charge and come out to the ranch. Is seven ok?" Natasha asked.

"Sounds perfect." Beau kissed her nose. "Go back to sleep. I'll eat my breakfast and let myself out. I'll see you tonight."

"Okay, get home safe," Natasha said.

"Tasha."

"Yeah?"

"I like how you smell and look when you wake up."

"Um, thanks."

Natasha moved quickly down the hall back to her bedroom and closed the door. She was flush with happiness at his words and wondered if this could be the start of something with Beau. After all these years, she didn't want to hope and have it dashed away. She decided to play it cool and see where it went. That didn't mean when she fell back asleep her dreams weren't about Beau. Oh yes, they were, and the sexy images were high definition.

Chapter Two

By six in the evening, the lights of her truck hit the Huntsford town limits sign as she headed out to the Twin Falls ranch. All around the town and the outlying houses, she could see signs of the holiday. The mayor's tree lined home had each tree filled with lights. Mr. Maynard's fencing had Merry Christmas spelled out in neon, and the steer's head he had on the gate wore a Rudolph nose. Mrs. Sims did her usual, transformed the pond on her property into an ice skating rink so that children and adults could skate. She even had her sons build a stand so she could give out hot chocolate and s'mores.

The holidays were a special time in the town, and everyone was filled with cheer. Except when she took the snowy turn to Twin Falls. Everything was dark. *Wait,* her eyes widened when she saw signs of the holiday at Cody's house. Could it be the twins finally decided to embrace the holidays again? On the other side of the corral, the only lights in Beau's house were on his patio. Well half of the duo at least, Natasha thought. She made the decision that she would bring Christmas to Beau. Before she went to Beau's house she pulled into Cody's driveway and knocked on the door.

His eyes widened in surprise when he opened the door. "Natasha, you're a little far out from Huntsford."

"I'm having dinner with Beau," she explained. "Hey, do you have any of those decorations left?"

"Um, Kaleena dragged them out, but a few boxes are left. You know how my mom used to decorate," Cody said. "What are you going to do with them?"

"I'm decorating Beau's place," she answered.

Cody looked at her somberly. "Does he know that?"

"I'd like to see him stop me," Natasha muttered and asked. "How is it you're all in the Christmas spirit, and why is Beau so hardheaded?"

Cody sighed. "Honestly, Kaleena is here, and she makes a difference. You have to understand Beau was the one who got the call and him and Dad had argued the night before. He felt as if he never got the chance to apologize to Dad, and its been eating him up all these years. He was going to talk him on Christmas Day, and it was too late in his eyes."

"Doesn't he understand that Mr. Everett would never hold a stupid argument in his head? He died loving both of you," Natasha said.

"I know that and you know that. Maybe it's time you show him love can surpass anything," Cody said with a smile.

At Last

"Am I that obvious?" Natasha asked.

"No, but then Kaleena came back and proved that love can travel distances, and I don't intend to let that pass by," Cody said. "And you shouldn't either. I'll help get the boxes in your truck."

Five minutes later, she was leaving Cody's driveway and making the small turn to Beau's house. The twins lived in two separate homes, because they needed space. They were two very different people. Cody was more laid back with a streak of dominance a mile wide. Beau was always the bad boy type, who wasn't afraid to punch first and ask questions after. The twins were like opposite sides of the same coin. She parked her truck close to the steps leading up to Beau's patio and grabbed a box from the back of her truck. He was opening the door by the time she reached it with a questioning look in his face.

"What's in the box?" Beau asked.

"Christmas decorations from Cody's place, some of your mom's stuff," Natasha answered as she walked past him.

"Why?" Beau asked.

Natasha put the box down on the floor in the hallway and turned with her hand on her hips. "Because you, Beau Everett, are a Grinch and you've gotten rid of Christmas. I'm bringing it back to your house." She pointed a finger at him when he opened his mouth to speak. "Shut it, not one word about it not happening because I won't take no for an answer. You're going to like it, and this year you're celebrating Christmas."

"Is that an order?" Beau asked, and she heard the amusement in his voice.

"Yes, it is," she replied.

"Ok, I have a counter offer. I'll do all the Christmas stuff if you give me one thing." He stepped closer, and his voice was like a husky caress over her skin. "Something I've been wanting for a long time now."

Natasha suddenly felt like her breath was caught in her chest. She looked up at the tall, sexy man who had become the star of every wet dream she had. "And what would that be?"

He grasped her waist and pulled her against his hard body. "A kiss and a chance to court you right and proper. Since I came home, I've been thinking we've been mind fucking each other for a long time now. Let's bring it to reality."

"This sounds like blackmail," she said softly

"Do you mind?" Beau asked.

"Hello, no, it's about damn time. I thought I would have to practically rip my shirt open and show you my boobs for you to get the hint," she replied.

Beau tilted his head back and laughed before saying, "I'd like to add that to my Christmas list. God, Natasha, you are unlike any woman I've ever met. Piss and vinegar in a creamy chocolate package."

"Kiss me and find out what I taste like," she invited.

At Last

Beau didn't need hesitate. His mouth met hers, and with a little moan, she opened under the onslaught of his kiss. His tongue penetrated her mouth, and she felt almost drunk on his taste. She had waited so long to be in his arms like this, to be held the way he holding her now.

He lifted his head and stared into her eyes before giving a long, low groan and taking her lips in a kiss again. He turned quickly, and Natasha found herself pressed up against the wall. Lord, the man was making her melt with one kiss, and his tongue was doing delicious things inside her mouth.

Beau raised his head and murmured. "That was so worth the wait. I felt like I got my gift early."

Whew, Natasha thought and waited for the fog of desire to clear from her brain. *I need to step back just a little before I'm naked in the tinsel and covered in Christmas lights.*

She giggled at the thought and poked him in the chest. "Rein in the sweet talk, cowboy. There will be no getting into these pants tonight."

Beau chuckled. "You are such a tease."

"Hey, it doesn't mean you can't get in them some other night. Just play your cards right." She slipped from between him and wall and went back to the door. "Come help me with this stuff, and then you promised me food."

"I did do that, so let's get this show on the road. I've got a prime rib in the broiler and russet potatoes with a vegetable medley." Beau winked at her. "For dessert there is my famous chocolate killer cake, guaranteed to make you want me naked before the night is through."

"I bet you say that to all the girls," Natasha said dryly.

"You're the only one that counts," Beau said softly from behind her.

He probably didn't mean for her to hear it, but she did, and a warm flush travelled along her body. Natasha had to top herself from doing her little happy dance at the front door. With his help, she got everything into the house, and then she convinced him to walk out near the woods behind his house to cut a fir tree.

"The things I do for you," he grumbled good-naturedly, but he used the small power saw to cut down the medium sized tree.

Together they dragged it back into the house, and he found a tree stand in the closet under the stairs so they could get it to stand upright.

"I'll use one of my dad's old tricks to keep it from drying out," Beau said.

"What's his trick because mine is already starting to drop needles on the carpet," Natasha said.

"He puts two cans of Pepsi in with the water. The syrup keeps the pines from falling. I'll grab the sodas, check on dinner, and be right back."

"You're being awfully good about all this," Natasha commented.

At Last

He stopped and considered what she said and then grinned. "I guess you kissed the scrooge out of me."

Natasha laughed as he walked away and started pulling lights from the box. They were the older kind of string lights, the bigger lighted bulbs from the seventies and still in pristine condition. The ornaments were delicate glass, and some were wood. She picked up two pairs of booties that were carved from wood. Santa Claus was painted on each pair and snowflakes. Beau and Cody's names were etched on each. Natasha knew that Mr. Everett carved them for his boys. She cradled them gently in her hands and hung them on the tree first. It felt right. She felt a kind of peace settle over her. Somewhere out there, his parents were happy.

"Two Pepsis, and look I brought us some wine." Beau came through the door and stood beside her. He looked at the ornaments on the tree and reached out to touch them gently. "I forgot about these. Mom used to hang them on the tree each year. I remember bringing home Susie Marsh for dinner one holiday, and Mom showed them off to her."

"Susie Marsh and her extra tight sweaters," Natasha said in irritation. "Like the whole school needed to know about her and her damn D-cups."

Beau laughed. "Every boy wanted those D cups, and I got them."

"And this very pleasant night has been put into the

garbage disposal," Natasha muttered and turned away from the tree to rummage through the box. "Men only remember the girls with the tits and not the one who helped get them through Algebra even though she was two years behind."

He grabbed her by the shoulders and tried to give her a hug. "Natasha, your mother would not even let me near you. I was going off to college and you were a junior. Trust me I tried. And in Huntsford trying to keep a secret about us being together would be impossible. So I bided my time until you got of age. Who knew you'd run away to the big city."

"True, and my parents would have skinned you alive," she admitted grudgingly. "But you sure took your time showing interest."

"Hey, you could've made a move," Beau pointed out.

"Proper girls do not chase boys," Natasha said primly.

"Who got caught sneaking out the window to go drink High Rider by the creek with Jonathan Berns, or joy riding with Tommy Pierce in his firebird?" Beau asked.

"Well then let's put it this way, they were fun and that was child's play. You should chase me, Beau, and when you catch me, it will be well worth it." Natasha put her hand on her hip. "And yes, if you're wondering, Beau Everett, yes, I'm just that damn good."

"You are something remarkable," Beau said. "And I can't wait to see where it leads. Let's drink some wine, trim the tree, and eat some dinner. Besides, Susie's D-cups were fake."

Natasha jumped up and down with glee. "I knew that skank stuffed her bra."

"Even better, it was a water bra, and it sprung a leak." Beau grinned.

She laughed. "Oh I so want to hear that story. She comes to Huntsford every Thanksgiving, trying to be posh. It would be great to say something snippy and take that nose from up in the air."

"You are a wicked woman, Natasha," Beau said.

"You betcha cowboy boots I am."

The rest of the night they decorated his house using his mom's keepsakes and then sat down to a dinner in front of the fireplace. Later while watching a movie, they ate his sinfully decadent chocolate cake and somewhere after midnight, she fell asleep snuggled beneath a thick afghan on his wide couch.

"I've got to head home," she muttered sleepily when he lifted her into his arms, still wrapped in the afghan.

Beau kissed her gently. "Uh-huh, it's my turn to play host, and besides, I want to hold you in my bed."

"Okay, but no hanky-panky," she said and closed her eyes as he walked upstairs.

Beau laid her on the bed and pulled her boots and jeans off before climbing in bed beside her. Natasha turned into his arms easily as if she was always meant to be there. Nothing felt more right than feeling his arms around her or the warm skin of his chest against her cheek.

Chapter Three

Natasha woke up in Beau's large bed, completely alone but with a smile. Some time in the night her sweater was making her overheat, so she sat up and whipped it off. She felt his soft kisses on her shoulder before he left and snuggled under his thick blankets when she missed his body curved in behind her. She sat up and stretched before getting out of bed and walking over to look out his bedroom window. It faced the coral, and she saw him standing alone in the snow with a bridle in his hand. On the other side of the coral stood a magnificent horse. Even from where she stood she saw the tense stand off between man and beast. Beau moved toward the animal with slow steps. She knew he was talking to the horse because she'd seen him work before.

The horse bent his head and scraped its hoof against the snow-covered ground. Beau got close enough to run his hand down its ink black coat and dropped the bridle on the ground. He pulled a brush out of the big pocket of his thick coat and ran it down the animal's muscled flanks. Talking to it gently while grooming the animal was all about building trust. Natasha knew he would never use the bridle on the ground, not today at least. He wanted the horse to get used to seeing him with it before he slipped it onto the horse's head. Natasha watched for a little while longer and then headed downstairs to make some breakfast. It was Sunday. Deena would have locked up the night's restaurant and bar tally in the safe in the back office. It was a few days before Christmas, and she planned to have some fun for a change.

Beau came in through the backdoor and stomped his feet on the thick brush mat. "Hey, muffin, you're up early."

Natasha almost choked on the sip of coffee she took while she stood at the stove. "Muffin?"

"I was trying it out," Beau commented as he hung up his coat.

"It's funny because I do have corn muffins in the oven," she replied and turned back to the stove where she cooked sausage links. "So are we doing this?"

He walked up behind her and wrapped his arms around her waist. "Doing what exactly?"

"Me, you, us," Natasha said.

"You slept in my bed. I think that says something," Beau said.

"Does it?" she replied. "Here I am cooking in your kitchen, wearing your T-shirt and sweat pants."

"Which looks great on you," he added.

At Last

"And after a few kisses a girl needs to know where she stands," she continued. "Thanks, they are huge on me but comfy, and they smell like you, so that's nice."

Beau kissed her neck. "Thanks for the compliment."

"You're welcome."

Beau took the heavy cast iron skillet off the stove's heating element and put it on the back burner. He turned her gently by the shoulders to face him and looked into her eyes.

"Me and you, well we're an us. We've always been an us." Beau ran his fingers along her lips. "Damn, girl, maybe I've pussyfooted around you so long that we've got used to the dance. You stand with me in my arms, tasting my kiss and knowing that my feelings, my desire, is for you and you alone."

"Ok, so we're solid," Natasha said.

"Like gold bars, muffin." She crunched up her nose and he asked, "Still no?"

"I don't think anyone could look at me and see *muffin*. How about sexy wild thing?" Natasha teased.

"I can do that." Beau grinned. "Do you need to be back in town today?"

"Nope. I'm closed until the party Christmas night."

"Then you'll spend it here with me, right?" Beau asked. "I'm embracing the holidays for you. Remember, you kind of threatened me."

"I'll spend it with you. It's the best Christmas present

I could ever have." Natasha stood up on her tiptoes to kiss him.

"Ok, let's eat breakfast, and then you relax around the house. I have a small surprise I'm planning for later I need to set up." Beau winked. "Do you need any help?"

"Hey, you can't say something like that and then just ask for breakfast." She pushed him to sit at the kitchen table and began to fix him a plate. "Sit. I've almost got it ready. I may run into town later to grab some Christmas dinner fixings. Your fridge is sorely lacking anything edible."

"Ok, then grab my ATM card and get anything you need. I'll be back to pick you up by four or so," he said.

"You're being awfully secretive." She put two plates on the table and sat down close to him.

"You'll like it, trust me." Beau broke into one of the corn muffins. "Thanks for this. I usually have cereal for breakfast."

"Hmm, yet you seem so well fed." Natasha poked at his shoulder. "Remind me to cook for you often."

"I won't complain. Cody gets tired of me poaching his food. He goes to the store regularly for his frozen dinners."

Natasha laughed, and they ate their breakfast. Beau helped clean up the dishes and then took off on his secret mission. It was still too early to head into town. She planned to grab some clothes and a few more necessities

At Last

for spending Christmas at Beau's, including her sexy undies. Till then she prattled around his house noticing where he extended out from the original ranch house to make his home. She passed the door that was built in under the stairs. Natasha fiddled with the knob and found it unlocked.

There were boxes inside, dusty and old. Curiosity got the best of her, and she pulled them out one by one. It was past mementoes from his parents, including boxes of old photographs. As Natasha looked through images of Beau and Cody growing up and of the family together at birthdays and holidays, she reminisced. She recalled one fourth of July picnic at Twin Falls when she was growing up. She found so many amazing photographs that she had a great idea. She gathered stacks of the best, the ones she could save, and rushed upstairs. Natasha showered and dressed in the clothes she wore the night before.

She'd do all the prettying up later at her place, but for now she had an idea for the perfect Christmas gift for Beau. Natasha got into her truck and drove down the icy driveway. At her house, she pulled on her apron and went into her dark room where she had her set up and graphics computer. If she was lucky and she got it all done today, her completed gift could be overnighted in at least twenty-four hours—just in time for Christmas morning.

Before she knew it, it was well past two, and she cursed beneath her breath. She'd spent extra time trying for perfection and was behind. She hit send for her final product and then took another shower and packed an overnight bag. She never took his ATM card. Instead she preferred to buy the things for dinner herself. She grinned and did her happy dance before heading outside and locking up her home. Beau Everett was finally her guy.

She did the shopping and got back to the ranch at four thirty. The skies were already getting dark as evening set in early in the winter months. When she walked into the kitchen carrying bags, Beau was sitting at the table drinking a cup of coffee.

"I thought you baled on me and I had to head into town and get you," Beau said.

She passed alongside him and bent to give him a quick kiss before putting her bags on the counter. "You can't get rid of me that easily. I went home to do a bit of work, something I forgot, and time got away from me."

"Holiday work, some lucky bastard is getting some boudoir photos for Christmas, huh?" He grinned. "Is it me?"

She winked at him. "You never know. Now what's this surprise?"

"Put on your warm gloves and coat. The horses are already saddled and ready to go," Beau said.

"Riding?" Natasha said curiously. "I heard the snow's going to be coming down pretty hard later on."

"We have until midnight or later, trust me. I'm a

At Last

Wyoming boy. We know the weather." Beau stood up and held out his hand. "Well, pretty lady, do you want to see your surprise or not?"

"Try and stop me." She put her hand in his.

Beau gave her a hard kiss before she bounded up the stairs to grab her gloves and scarf. She was back downstairs in a flash and ready to go.

"I haven't been on a horse in forever, so let's take a slow," she said as they stepped outside.

"Darling, I'll take as much time as you want," Beau drawled. "I saddled Beauty for you. She'll get you there, and I'll make sure your ride is slow and easy."

She got his double meaning, and it gave her a tingle low in her belly. She hoisted herself up on Beauty who was a gorgeous chestnut gelding, and he did the same on his horse. She followed him out the back fence to the trail covered in snow. The horses moved easily, and even though it was cold, she enjoyed the ride and looked around curiously as they ascended into Cloud Peak Mountain. Night made the sky turn from light blue to a dark blanket with stars as diamonds. There was no fear about getting home. Beau was one of the best trackers around. Natasha wondered where they were going until she saw the glitter of lights in the trees and candles on the rocks.

"What's all this?" she asked in amazement.

"It gets better," Beau called back to her.

"How did you get these lights to work without power up here?" Natasha asked.

"Battery operated, honey. Everything has batteries lately," he said.

They went on through an outcropping of rocks, and Natasha felt the area get warmer. What she saw next made her gasp in delight. Steam rose from water in a pool surrounded by rocks, some flat and wide as a bed. The high rocks of the mountains caused a natural buffer from the wind and snow, and insulated the warmth of the hot springs. In Wyoming the cavern in Cloud Peak Mountain where the hot springs sat was like a tropical oasis. Beau had managed to hang more lights off the rock, and by the pool sat a basket that held a bottle of wine and other goodies. In other words, Beau had created something magical just for her. She was so enthralled that she didn't even notice that'd he'd gotten off his horse until he came over to stand beside Beauty.

"Want to take a dip?" Beau asked softly.

"How did you…?" Natasha looked down at him with a smile. "I never knew this was here."

"No one does, sweetheart. This is on Everett land, a closely guarded secret." Beau helped her off Beauty and pulled her into his arms. "Not even the ranch hands know it's up here. Me and Cody actually keep it hidden creatively."

"It's amazing, so very beautiful, and you made it just perfect," Natasha breathed.

At Last

"For you. I've never done this for anyone else," he said softly, looking down at her.

"Well I've always heard those Everett boys are charmers. I guess you just proved the rumors right." She stepped away and pulled her gloves off and began to strip, sending his a coy look. "Are you just going to stand there or join me?"

"Oh I'm joining you." His voice was gruff with need.

She stepped naked into the hot spring pool, gasping in pleasure as the warmth ran up her feet to her body. The water was past warm but not so much so that it was painful. The water came up to her waist, and the rocks were smooth on the bottom of her feet as she walked farther into it. She crouched and sighed as she used her feet to push off the flat stone bottom and swam the length of the small pool.

"Oh this is marvelous," she cried out.

His arms came around her waist, and he brought her naked body against his. "No, you are. Watching you step into the pool was like watching a water nymph going back to her home."

She wrapped her arms around his neck. "I didn't know you were so eloquent with words."

"For you I would write a sonnet, m'lady." He kissed her neck. "You taste so much better than I ever dreamed."

"You dreamed of me?" Natasha asked and broke off with a moan. Oh his mouth felt wonderful on her skin.

"Always, I've woken up so hard and aching for you that I knew once could never be enough," Beau said. "I'd have to have you for the rest of my life."

"You can have me forever, Beau. That's all I ever wanted," Natasha said longingly. "Take me, Beau. Make me yours."

In the heat of the water, he claimed her lips, and nothing could compare to the flame he created inside her. Their eyes met, and Natasha lost herself in his blue-green. It was like being pulled by some invisible cord toward him. Everything in her life was pulling her inextricably to Beau and this moment in time.

"I want to see every ounce of pleasure on your face." His voice was deep and sexy.

Their lips met, her eyes closed, and Natasha made a soft sound of pleasure. She felt his cock pulse against her thigh. He pulled her closer, and Beau deepened the kiss until every nerve ending in her body screamed his name and begged to feel them joined completely. He broke the kiss, and with lips barely a millimeter away from each other, it was like sharing one breath, suspended in time. With his forehead against hers, he buried his hands in her wet hair, and she purred as he nuzzled her neck.

"I want you so damn much." Beau said the words on a moan. "You feel so perfect in my arms."

"I need you, Beau." She pressed kisses onto his face until he kissed her savagely.

At Last

A groan escaped his throat as they both succumbed to the desire that raged through them. *If the water weren't already hot, we'd make it boil,* Natasha thought, and as quickly as it filtered through her mind, it left. His taste, his masculine smell, it was all about Beau. Their clothes were long forgotten. The Christmas lights and candles danced across the surface of the water and along the ripples of water they caused. He lifted her into his arms and stepped from the pool with ease before he placed her on a thick blanket he'd spread out on the flat rock near the water's edge. Her passion emboldened her, and Natasha pulled him down for another kiss, and she slipped her tongue into his mouth. His moan of pleasure vibrated from his body to hers.

Beau changed their positions easily until she lay across his body, and she traced his calf with her toes. Natasha shivered as his hands moved from her hips to trace the dip of her back. He ran his hands down her thighs and pulled her legs apart to straddle him. She gasped as his hands roamed and massaged her body while her sex was open and ready to accept his cock. He was rock hard and throbbing against the warm sensitive flesh of her pussy. She undulated against him to tease him to take her. He groaned and took control of the kiss, burying his fingers in the thick tresses of her hair while devouring her lips.

He tore his mouth away from hers. "Jesus, I've wanted

you for years, and now I have you in my arms, it seems so unreal."

She looked into his eyes. "I've been in your arms in my dreams many nights, and this is so much better."

Her hands roamed over the strong contours of his shoulders. He filled his hands with the smooth chocolate globes of her breasts. Natasha moaned as she arched into his palms.

"Jesus, I have to taste you," he said gutturally. Beau buried his face between the twin mounds. "Do you like how my hands feel on you, the way I touch you?"

"Oh, yes, Beau," she whispered.

She took control and pushed him back with her hands on his shoulders. She licked and kissed her way down his body. His cock was already hard when she settled herself on her knees between his legs. She felt his eyes on her. The anticipation of her touch seemed to still his breath in his chest. She ran her hands down his rock hard stomach When she took his cock in her grasp and stroked, his breath hissed out. Beau's hips rose in time to each touch of her hand fisted around his rod.

Natasha bent low and took the head of his shaft into her mouth, and a low agonized moan left his lips. She took him deeper between her lips, and she felt him shudder. Natasha could taste the salty bite of his precome on her tongue. "Damn, I can't stand it," he said and pulled her roughly against his chest. He took her lips in a hunger filled kiss. He slipped his hand between their bodies to her pussy and found her slick and wet. He slid his two fingers deep inside her. Her body bucked against him, and a cry tore its way from her throat.

"That's it, that's what I want to hear. Say my name when you come," he growled.

She straddled his thighs, and he spread her legs wider to get more access to her snatch. He pushed his fingers deeper. "You are amazing to watch, so beautiful," he said. Natasha arched her back in enjoyment. She panted and braced her hands on his shoulders as pleasure swirled through her.

"Ride my fingers, darling," he coaxed her softly.

She felt his finger circle the sensitive nub of her clit in between the pink folds of her pussy. With every movement, she felt herself get more aroused and slicken with her own juice. She was unable to stop the tiny moans that escaped her parted lips.

"I'm going to come." Natasha's voice held urgency and almost a plea for release.

"Say my name. Let me hear my name on your lips while you come," he bit out harshly.

"Beau, oh God, Beau, yes," she cried out and shuddered.

He pressed his digits deeper inside her and pulled her close so he could take her hard nipples in his mouth. Her orgasm crashed though her, and she came with a scream.

While her body trembled, Beau didn't wait for her to catch her breath. He buried his cock inside her to the hilt and began to move urgently.

"Oh fuck," he said through gritted teeth.

Natasha wanted to bring him as much pleasure as he'd done for her. She began to move, writhing and undulating in a sensual dance. His fingers were deliciously clenched into the soft flesh of her hips, and he pulled her onto his shaft with deep purposeful movements. Their pace increased until a sheen of dampness formed on their bodies and not the warm water of the hot springs. He cupped her breasts and took her nipples into his mouth, feasting on her until she was like a piston, urgently riding his cock.

She kissed him fiercely. "Come with me, Beau. Don't let me go alone."

"Natasha, *God!*"

He thrust upward to meet her frenzied movements. The harshness of their breathing and the echo of their cries bounced off the rocks and mixed with the sound of trickling water. He pounded inside her, taking her higher than she had ever been in her life. Her name was a harsh primal cry wrung from his lips, and she called to him as her vision blurred when her orgasm took hold. He didn't stop. Beau moved inside her over and over again until he drove her to a second release. She fell against his chest, depleted of all her strength. Beau wrapped his arms

At Last

automatically around her, and she was cocooned in his loving embrace.

"Damn, I could die right now and be happy," he murmured and lay back against the blanket.

"I don't even want to move." Natasha sighed.

"Not even for this?" He reached down and brought a piece of rip fruit to her lips.

"Oh, but if you're feeding me then why should I move?" she pointed out.

"Good point. I'll feed you, and you lie there just looking desirable," Beau replied. "Then after, I'll make love to you again."

"Oh that sounds like a plan."

He put a piece of bread and cheese to her lips, and she bit into the soft morsel. There was something to be said for a hot springs oasis nestled in the middle of a wintery wonderland. More so because of the man she was with. He made it perfect.

Chapter Four

"Let's go ice skating," Beau said impulsively. "Mrs. Sims's place."

She raised he head and looked at him in surprise. "Beau Everett, did you really just say let's go skating?"

Natasha was lying across his lap, and he twirled her hair idly as they watched A Charlie Brown Christmas. He felt like a new man after only days of letting go and embracing the holidays and Natasha. Beau realized that he was just living day-to-day, year-to-year but not really living. One uncomplicated relationship to the next, working with the horses, buy and selling and bringing new foals into the world. Watching winter turn into spring and the pastures awash in yellow flowers, watching the new foals trot by with their mothers or helping Cody take cattle from the winter grounds or branding new calves.

It was all perfect and beautiful yet lonely because at the end of the day he went home alone. He'd drink a beer after grabbing a frozen dinner from Cody's house because it seemed useless to cook for himself alone. When that got monotonous, he'd head into town to eat at Razzlez just to

At Last

watch Natasha and never make a move. Keeping himself distanced from everyone because he didn't want to deal with the hurt of maybe losing them was the wrong move. His parents loved each other up to the day they died. He remembered seeing them walking hand-in-hand each evening by the coral. Damn it all if they wouldn't kick his ass for doing this to himself.

"Yeah, I said it." He chucked her gently under the chin. "I've decided to take a new stance on the holiday festivities thing. Two days before Christmas we should go drink some of Mrs. Sims's hot chocolate. I hear she mixes it with real chocolate."

"I don't know if I should be happy or terrified about your turn around, Scrooge," Natasha teased.

"Happy, ma'am, be very, very happy because you caused it." Beau bent over to kiss her nose. "So come on, sweetheart, let's take to the ice."

An hour later they were pulling onto Mrs. Sims's property and parking next to the rows of cars near the pond. Neither she nor Beau owned skates but decided to go anyway. The hot chocolate alone was enough to make them go out. Mrs. Sims always had extra pairs of skates she bought over the years, so she set them up just right.

"First Cody and then you come down to take a twirl on the ice,' Mrs. Sims commented. "I haven't seen you boys on my pond since you were teenagers. The mister and I can remember your momma and daddy doing the same thing, as if they were newlyweds skating and kissing. I miss those two."

Beau swallowed the lump in his throat. "Yeah, I do too. Thanks for the skates, Mrs. Sims."

"Go enjoy the ice, boy. It's about time I seen you and Natasha here," she called out to them.

"Does everybody in this town know we've got the hots for each other?" Beau asked as they sat down on one of the benches close to the pond.

"Oh yeah, I think there is an underground betting pool going on at Razzlez," Natasha said as she laced up her skates. "They think I don't know, but I put in a fifty that this Christmas we'd get together."

Beau looked at her amazed. "You're with me for a bet?"

Natasha laughed and skated away. "I'm kidding, you nut. Get out here and glide."

"Oh I thought I was just a cheap trick to you." Beau followed her out to the ice. On a horse he was a magician. On the ice, Beau had to find his sea legs. Maybe skating was a bad idea.

"You would never be just a trick to me, stud." Natasha skated into his arms. "You're my stallion, and later I plan to ride you and break you, baby."

Beau felt his cock harden in response. "Don't say that now. I might have you in the flat bed of my truck freezing my ass off trying to fuck you."

At Last

"You forget. I'd be on top." She kissed him.

Natasha's words were like a punch to his libido, the girl always the one thing could make him rock hard in an instant. He remembered he'd asked her dad if he could date her. Yeah, he had just turned eighteen, and she was only fifteen, but he gave it a go. Mr. Quinlan threatened to beat him bloody if he came anywhere near his daughter. Then he'd just left for college and lost his parents that same December. She'd gone off to the big city and never really came home since her parents left Huntsford for Florida's warmer climate. But here they were finally together, and her fiery personality could get him hot and bothered instantly. Beau knew he'd loved her from the start, and right now in that place with her, it was like a gust of wind clearing out the stale air of the past.

"Hey, Natasha, looking good!"

Beau watched as Nate skated up to Natasha and picked her up in a hug. Beau folded his fist at his side and was ready to punch Nate's face in. He was the town's one and only insurance adjustor and known to be a ladies man. His dark hair was ruffled by the wind, and while he was working his way through the single and not so single women in Huntsford, Beau knew he'd always had Natasha in his sights. She had always refused him.

"Nate, take your hands off me. I didn't give you permission to touch me," Natasha said. "You act like we're close and you're definitely too touchy-feely."

"Awww, sweetie, don't be that way. I thought maybe we could give another date a go." Nate grinned. Beau wanted to punch him all the more.

"You dated him?" Beau came up beside them and put his hand around her shoulder before saying casually, "She said move your hands. Don't make me break them."

"It was one date, one that I won't be repeating . . . ever," Natasha said, and he heard the sourness in her voice.

"So you and Beau are...?" Nate grinned. "You got to her before I could."

Beau rolled his eyes. Nate was always a clueless fool. He thought he was God's gift to women even though that myth was proven untrue over and over again.

"Let me point out that you would never have gotten me," Natasha said. "You are slimy, and after what you did to poor Keith and his wife, I doubt you will ever be under the blankets of another woman's bed in Huntsford. You are the lowest of the low."

"I'm kind of out of the loop. What did he do to Keith and Jessica?" Beau asked.

"Oh, it didn't get out to Twin Falls?" Natasha asked. "Let me enlighten you. Nate here decided to blackmail Jess into sleeping with him. Keith couldn't pay the insurance premiums, and he told her to trade was best. Mister Nate then let the policy lapse even though he was sleeping with her, and they almost lost everything. When she found out, Jessica was livid and told Keith everything. Jessica is pregnant, and the scum told Keith the baby was his even though it wasn't. His spite almost broke them up. Even though Jess was trying to save her husband's business, Keith still blamed her. All because of this pond scum."

"I should hit you in the face right now." The burn of his anger almost overwhelmed Beau. "Jess is one of the most innocent women I know. That girl still believes in rainbows and unicorns."

"Hey, she could've said no." Nate sneered. "I think she taught me a few tricks."

Beau raised his fist, but Natasha stopped him. "He's not worth it, Beau. He'll get his. Karma is a bitch."

"But I would feel so much better," Beau murmured. "No woman should have to deal with him in their presence."

"I'm here with Deena," Nate said smugly.

"I'll be fixing that shortly," Natasha replied. "That girl's been here for less than a year and tends to keep to herself and out of gossip. She doesn't know about you, but I will be telling her everything."

Natasha waved to Deena, and when the young woman came over, Natasha linked their arms. "Let's go have a hot chocolate. I've got some things to tell you."

Nate tried to block them from leaving. "Hey now, she came with me."

Beau put his hand on Nate's shoulder and squeezed none too lightly. "Let's leave the ladies, shall we? I still want to hit you badly."

Nate pushed away from Beau and skated across the ice. On the other side of the pond, he sat on one of the benches to take off his skates. He stalked to his elaborately pimped out truck and drove away without looking back for his date. Beau turned and found Natasha and Deena sitting near the hot chocolate stand. He let them talk for a bit while he ordered his own drink and three cinnamon rolls. He gave each lady one of the sweet treats and sat quietly while Natasha gave Deena the rundown about one of the town's gigoloes.

I can't believe I almost took that piece of shit home." Deena made a disgusted sound in the back of her throat.

"He took off in his truck," Beau commented.

Deena sighed. "Just my luck I let him pick me up. Can you guys give me a ride back to my place?"

"Can we, Beau?" Natasha asked. "It's close to the restaurant."

"I'd never leave a lady stranded." Beau grinned. "My mom raised me right."

Deena chuckled. "Are there any more like him?"

"He has a twin, but he's already taken," Natasha said.

"Bummer, all the good ones are taken or gay, and then we're left with men like Nate." Deena laughed.

"Never. There're some good guys in Huntsford."

At Last

Natasha stood and so did Deena. "You just have to be selective. We'll talk about it at work sometime."

Deena laughed. "Ok."

Beau drove, and they got Deena home safely before heading back to Twin Falls. When they got inside, Beau lit a fire so they could warm up. His cellphone went off just as Natasha was coming in the room with two brandy snifters in her hands. He looked at the read out, and it was Cody. He never refused a call from his brother.

"Hey, C, what's up?" Beau asked. He listened for a moment and replied. "Sure I can help with that. Tell Bruce I hope he feels better."

"Hey, tell Cody and Kaleena to come over for Christmas Dinner," Natasha said. "We girls can get to know each other."

"Did you hear that, Cody? My girl wants to meet your girl," Beau said with humor in his voice. He looked at Natasha. "He and Kaleena will be here, four ok?"

"Sounds perfect," Natasha said.

"Ok, bro, see you Christmas Day and then work the day after," Beau said. He hung up and joined Natasha who had settled herself in front of the fire's warm embers. "It seems we're having a family dinner."

She gave him a sidelong glance. "How do you feel about that? I mean it's been so long and you're…"

"It's fine," Beau said gently. "You're right, my mom and dad wouldn't want me to live like this. I don't know how I let it get this far. After awhile it felt so much easier than actually dealing with the issues."

"Do you want to talk about it?" Natasha asked.

"I'm not ready yet," Beau said and cupped her cheek before kissing her. "Right now all I want to think about is you."

Natasha put her drink down on the stone fireplace surface and straddled his waist as he was leaning back against the sofa. "Is this where I try to break my stallion?"

"I'll buck and won't submit lightly," Beau said huskily.

Natasha grabbed the lapels of his button down shirt and gave him a look. She bit her lower lip, and he wanted to soothe the soft flesh with his tongue. Natasha ripped his shirt open and exposed his chest. She bent her head and nipped gently at his nipple. Beau groaned and leaned his head back. He'd let her play for a moment, but then Beau planned to give her the ride of her life.

The next kiss seared her into his senses until nothing mattered but Natasha. Stroking and massaging her body made him hunger for her even more. They undressed quickly, catching teasing kisses or a nip of tender skin here and there as they did. Beau delved his hand between her legs and cup the mound of her pussy. His finger stroked and teased between the wet slit before he penetrated her with his finger, and she moaned against his mouth. He loved every sound she made when he made her purr like a kitten or whimper in need.

He lifted his head and watched her as he used his fingers to please her. He loved the way she felt warm and wet, the way her body accepted his touch. "Damn, you're so tight and wet."

"Oh please," she moaned.

"Please what?" His husky voice was right by her ear. He wanted her ask him to please her. "Tell me what you need, baby girl."

"Make me come," she pleaded.

"Look at me," he ordered. "I want to see you go over that edge."

Beau was drawn to her chocolate brown gaze. In his heart, she was already his, and Beau loved how she opened herself up to him completely. "Oh, Beau," she cried out, and he groaned in response. She made him want to roar his pleasure and shout to the world that she was in his arms, his woman. He deliberately slowed down his movements wanting to draw out her pleasure as long as he could. It made her more frenzied, and Beau felt himself losing control.

He kept that pace until she begged. "Harder, I need more!"

Beau laughed. "Very bad girl, are you going to come for me?"

"Yes, oh yes." She panted and pumped her hips against his hand.

Natasha gave a small scream, and he felt her pussy give up its bounty. *Yes,* he thought in delight, reveling in how her body bowed and tensed in passion. His cock was hard as steel and ached almost painfully. She stroked his length, and Beau groaned, loving the feel of her grasp around his rod. They were both striving to bring each other pleasure. Beau slipped another finger inside her, sliding them deeper and faster, and he watched as her head fell back as ecstasy. He knew her excitement was building by the way she stroked him. He gritted his teeth trying to find the restraint he needed.

She spread her legs wider, taking more of his fingers. Their lips so close yet not touching, and with every breath she expelled, he took it in while he manipulated her clit. He wanted to see her come again. Her hips rose and fell in earnest.

"Oh, stop. I can't stand it!" She pushed against his hand.

Beau stopped her. "Oh no, sweetheart, you're going to come for me. I'll have all of it, every last ounce of pleasure I can wring from your body."

She reached the pinnacle of desire, and her body drew tight like a bow. She came with a scream, and Beau watched in delight as she orgasmed with his name on her lips. She lay with her eyes closed, pliant while he sucked at her breasts.

"My turn," Natasha said breathlessly as she rolled

At Last

over and crawled to him. "I want to taste you."

She pushed him back and took his hard length in her hand. As she stroked him, Beau arched and tensed at her touch. She could ask him to climb a mountain or kill a bear, and he'd do it. Just to feel her and have her taste on his tongue.

A low moan escaped his lips at her ministrations. She licked the tip of his cock slowly then ran her tongue down the erect shaft. She gently nipped at the sensitive skin of his balls before soothing and liking them with her tongue. Natasha worked her way back up his cock and took inch by pleasurable inch into her mouth. She sucked his cock and swirled her tongue around the head. Beau grabbed her head and slid his cock in and out between her lips.

"You do that so good, baby," he groaned.

His body tightened and tensed, each motion of her tongue causing him unbearable delight. He pulled away suddenly breathing harshly.

"If I didn't stop you, I'd come in your mouth," Beau said.

He pulled her to her knees and bent her over in front of him. He rubbed his cock up and down the wet slit, and Natasha moaned in excitement. He knew exactly what she felt because he wanted to sink himself inside her and blur the lines of reality. With one smooth thrust, he filled her and surged forward once, then twice, making her cry out his name.

"Ah, Tasha, you feel so damn good," he muttered.

"Don't tease me. Fuck me hard," she begged.

He couldn't have gone slow even if he tried. Beau pumped into her at a feverish pace, and he felt the flames of her desire lap at him. The noises their bodies made as he took her were primal. He reached around to cup her breasts and brought her off her hands to just being on her knees while he fucked her.

"Yes, yes, yes." Natasha chanted the words over and over again.

She came hard. He felt it course through her body. He'd never felt like this before, didn't know her body could reach such heights, her pussy so wet it ran down his cock.

"Baby, I can't hold back," he groaned. His balls tightened, and he gritted his teeth in pleasurable agony.

"Oh, Beau, fill me." She reached between her legs to cup his balls and squeezed them.

That sensation was his undoing. " Fuck, yes!" With a loud harsh cry, he grabbed her hips and pumped into her mercilessly. He threw his head back and opened his mouth to a silent yell as his come filled her with each thrust. He moved until nothing was left, and they both slumped to the carpet, sweaty, damp, and breathless.

"Did I break the stallion?" Natasha teased.

"Oh honey, I'm yours. Grab the rope and tie me up." Beau chuckled.

At Last

"That'll be next time," she purred.

"Lord, woman, you may kill me, but I'll go into that sweet night blissfully content." He sighed.

"Oh no, Beau Everett, I plan to keep you around for a long time," Natasha said softly. "I don't even want to think about you not...."

He cut her off with a gentle kiss. "You won't be losing me."

"Good, remember that," Natasha said firmly.

"I plan on it, so should I carry you upstairs to bed?" Beau asked.

"How about we grab that afghan and we cuddle by the fire for awhile?" she suggested.

"You have the most amazing ideas." Beau pulled the afghan down and wrapped it around them.

"Stick with me, kid, and I'll show you the stars," she murmured and kissed his chest.

"You already have," he said in a quiet voice.

A cuddle by the fire turned into them sleeping there the entire night. Beau rose at his usual time and looked down at the sleeping woman. Natasha curled up like a kitten and continued to sleep. His heart filled with love, and it almost overwhelmed him. *Just a little longer*, he thought and lay back beside her. Just a little longer to hold onto the woman he loved.

Chapter Five

Christmas Eve brought snow and the threat of a major blizzard. Still the Fed Ex truck made it in time, and she had her gift for Beau. She looked out at the fluffy white snowflakes falling lazily to the ground and then to the gift she'd carefully wrapped that sat in her lap. Soon the snow would be so heavy she wouldn't be able to see the circular hedge pots in the driveway. Beau was outside in the stables taking care of his horses. But when she saw him running across the driveway, she knew something was wrong. Beau usually walked with purposeful strides, never in a hurry to get anywhere but always making it in time. If he was running, there was a reason.

Not even caring about a coat, she opened the door and stepped outside. "Beau, what's wrong?"

"Midnight is down. It's colic. I'm going to get Cody to help," Beau said.

"I saw his truck pull out a little bit ago. He and Kaleena must be out," Natasha said. "Can I help?"

"Come with me." He didn't even wait for an answer. He moved back across the ground at a dead run.

At Last

Natasha ran inside and grabbed her coat before sitting in the kitchen to lace up her boots. She sprinted out the door and made a beeline for the stables. She could hear him soothing the animal, so she moved toward his voice. On the floor of the stall, in the midst of fresh hay, laid the horse she'd seen him working with in the corral. She didn't know much about horses except that when they were lying down it was bad.

"We've got to get him up and walking. Lying down and thrashing his legs like he is, he can twist his intestines," Beau said. "He won't want to get up, but we have to make him."

How do we do that? she wondered but didn't say it out loud. The horse thrashed not only because it was in pain but also because he hadn't been tamed as yet, which made it definitely more dangerous.

"We're not going to hurt you," Beau said calmly and stroked the beast's long neck. "Let me help you. Midnight, you rascal you've been breaking out of your stall and overeating."

Beau started to hum a song she didn't recognize, but it seemed to soothe the horse. He slipped a bridle on the horse's head, and soon they had him up and walking the length of the stables. Fifteen-minute intervals and then they'd put him back into the stall to rest. Each time Midnight wanted to lay down, they didn't let him. Beau was always with him and giving him medicine or gently talking to the horse. He loved his animals, and the worry on his face was evident until the tide turned and he could tell Midnight was out of danger. Still they kept on and did it for hours until the horse stopped sweating and seemed at ease. The breaking of Midnight wasn't meant to happen in the corral but in his stall being cared for by his owner. Beau patted the horse's neck as it looked out over the stall door.

"No food for you, Midnight Ink," Beau crooned. "We'll let your stomach settle." He moved away and held out his hand to Natasha. "Ready to go inside, honey?"

Natasha laced her fingers with his and teased, "You smell like horse."

Beau laughed and wrinkled his nose. "You do too, Ms. Quinlan. We should shower."

"Yeah, we should and then nap," Natasha said.

"If I could amend that statement—shower, hot sex, and then nap," Beau said. "I find that I get horny as hell after a crisis."

"I think I could fit you in," Natasha purred. "Race you to the water."

The shower was hot. Steam filled the cubicle as hot passionate kisses were dispensed, and slick hands lathered each other's bodies. Natasha was amazed at how his hands, so rough and calloused, could ignite such a fire in her body. These were a working man's hands that fixed fences and baled hay. They were hands that labored to

At Last

break horses or rope cattle. Yet the way he touched her with such gentleness, care, and infused with passion was her undoing.

He wrapped her legs around his waist as they left the shower still soaking wet. He put her on the bed, uncaring that they were slick with water. His hands cupped the globes of her breasts, and he engorged himself on her hard nipples. Natasha moaned his name and held his head. Beau lifted her easily, and she was always amazed at how tiny and fragile he made her feel. He lay on the bed and brought her over him. Her nipples were in his mouth once more, and Natasha whimpered in pleasure. She arched her back, pushing more of her smooth globe deeper into his mouth, wanting more. The urge to be devoured by him overrode every other thought.

"Oh, Beau, please more," she moaned.

Natasha could feel his thick cock between her legs making her want and ache to have him inside her. She rubbed against him, the friction on her clit causing sweet pleasure, and he groaned in response.

"Lord, girl, I'll fuck you hard if you don't stop doing that," he muttered.

"Do it. Fill me and fuck me hard," she begged feverishly.

"Oh no, honey. I like to take my time on each and every curve," he growled. "I want to have your taste on my tongue."

"Make me come with your mouth." Natasha climbed off him and lay back on the pillows.

She panted, not feeling like she was getting enough air. She spread her legs and exposed her sex to him, and the heat from his eyes made her juice flow. With a guttural moan, he buried his face between her legs and tasted the core of her sex. Her back arched, and pleasure lanced through her like a bolt of energy. She screamed and clutched the damp sheets beneath her. Beau licked and sucked at her clit before she felt his fingers circle the sensitive flesh of her entrance. He slid his fingers inside her over and over again. She cried out, and she moved her hips, pressing herself more intimately against his lips and seeking hands. She slipped her hands into his thick hair and bucked against him. She could feel herself reaching for the pinnacle of her release. He fucked her harder with his fingers until she came with such force that her body tensed and she lost her breath. Natasha cried out as each sensation assaulted her body, and she came apart under his mouth.

"I want you inside me. Now, damn it. Beau, *now*," she demanded.

"Oh yes, yes." His voice was a harsh whisper, and he pulled her over him and brought her down hard onto his cock.

He was so long and hard he touched places inside her that made her shudder and whimper his name. Half the

At Last

time she didn't know if she could take him all, yet knew that she craved every inch.

"Damn, you so tight. I need more of you." He pulled her hips down again hard and sent himself deeper inside her. She cried out in ecstasy, and she undulated on the object of her pleasure. Beau groaned and buried his face in the valley of her breasts. His hand reached around and gripped her shoulders pulling her hard against him. The repetitive movements made her tremble until she screamed his name, and his voice combined with hers in a guttural cry.

"God, yes!" She grabbed his hair and pulled his head from her breasts. They kissed long, hard, and passionately before she pleaded, "Come with me, Beau. Come with me."

He pumped himself inside her in deep strokes, pushing himself to the hilt. Her hips rose to meet his every thrust, and she tightened her legs around him. They were glossy with sweat, and she could hear their bodies meet with wet, slick sounds.

"God, I love you. God, I love you so much," he ground out between clenched teeth.

"I'm yours forever, Beau. I love you too," she gasped out.

It was as if the dam broke inside her, and Natasha screamed as her body shook from the intensity of her orgasm. Beau called her name and pounded himself inside her until he followed her into his own release. Their bodies heaved as they tried to catch their breath. Natasha lost track of the frantic beats of her heart and just kept her eyes closed until it at last resumed a normal rhythm.

"I think I need another shower. The last one was dirty," she murmured.

"Hmmm." He sighed in contentment before moving toward her plaint body. "God, I do love you, darling."

"I love you too, Beau," she said. "Is it time for the nap part of the program?"

"Not quite yet," he said and rolled them both until she was beneath him.

His cock was hard and ready again. He filled her once more and began a slow rhythm that she matched easily. A deep, lingering kiss and then he took one of her nipples in his mouth and sucked it deeply between his lips.

"Oh, God, yes," she moaned and lifted her hips higher to take him deeper.

He kissed her long, slow, and deep before giving her a wicked grin. "When it comes to you, baby, my appetite will never be satisfied."

Natasha gave in to the need once more and let it consume her. It was after frozen pizza in bed and ice cream that she finally settled in for that nap—in the arms of the man she loved a few hours before Christmas morning.

At Last

* * * *

She smelled cinnamon, and it tickled her nostrils, tempting her to awaken. She felt around the bed for her man, her Beau. He was gone of course, and she gave a husky laugh. Natasha knew she better get used to it. Men like Beau got up before the sun, but the smell of cinnamon was the curious thing that had her rolling out of bed. *What is he up to?*

Natasha knew exactly where to find his T-shirts and sweats, and soon she was clothed heading downstairs. She found quite a sight waiting for her. Breakfast had been set up in front of the fireplace close to the Christmas tree. Beau stood there wearing a Santa's hat and a fake beard. He held two cups of coffee and a big grin. Natasha paused at the bottom of the steps and took it in before laughing in amazement.

"What's all this? Santa in my house wearing a T-shirt and flannel pajama bottoms?" she asked stepping into the room.

"Santa decided to stay and visit with his favorite elf," Beau said. "Come here and give old Santa a kiss."

"I thought after last night, Santa might still be asleep." Natasha walked into his arms.

He kissed her gently. "I wanted to do something nice for my favorite girl."

"One second, I have to get you my gift." Natasha ran

to the window seat and picked up her package from the cushions. She came back to sit close to him at their makeshift Christmas breakfast picnic. "Here, this is for you. Merry Christmas, Beau."

He looked down at the package in his lap and then to her. "When did you have time to shop?"

"I didn't. I kinda of threw this together," Natasha said. "Open it."

He tore the paper off and looked down at the hunter green book in his hand. He traced his finger over the golden embossed letters that spelled out the family name, *The Everett Family*. She watched him as he opened the book to reveal its contents. Pictures of his family, fragments of time forever saved in a book she put together. His parents wedding pictures, them in front of the newly built house, Beau and Cody's first day home as babies, first birthdays, and family picnics. Beau standing with his blue ribbon at his first rodeo, him and Cody in their football uniforms with *Go Huntsford Bulls* as the caption. She tried to capture every holiday and birthday and each special event of their lives. She watched him thumb through the pages carefully to the final picture of the family one year before his parents' death—that final Christmas with all of them by the Christmas tree.

"Where did you find these pictures?" he asked in a subdued tone.

"In the crawlspace under the stairs," Natasha

At Last

explained. "They were just under there gathering dust and disintegrating. I wanted to give you all the good memories in one place."

"You shouldn't have," he said.

"It wasn't any trouble. That day I went into town I took all the pictures, scanned them into my computer, and fixed the areas that were fading. Biff-bam-boom I built the book and sent it in to my designer, and he got it to me by Fed Ex yesterday before Midnight got sick." Her explanation was met with silent. "Beau?"

"I mean you shouldn't have literally. Natasha, what gave you the right to be searching through my house?" He stood.

"Really? You're getting upset because I made you a book of pictures of your family?" Natasha rose and put her hand on his shoulder. "Beau, talk to me."

"I told you I wasn't ready to talk, but you put yourself right in the thick of it trying to make me open up," he snapped. "Jesus, can't a man keep any part of himself?"

Natasha felt her irritation rise. "Whoa, hold up. How is my trying to do something nice for you prying into your dark and secret places? I never asked you to tell me anything."

"Well I put those there for a reason, so I wouldn't have to see them," Beau said. "This is doing nothing but…"

"But what?" Natasha demanded. "Making you

remember you had parents? Or even better that you had a happy life? Beau they died. They weren't erased from existence. Hiding the pictures in boxes behind closed doors won't change that."

"What would you know? Did you lose your parents? Did they die because you and your father were having a screaming match?" He turned tortured eyes to her.

"No, my father and mother are in Florida safe and sound," Natasha said. "But my mother, hell and me and my dad, have had seriously awful arguments. If they died tomorrow, I would never think they died not loving me. I knew your parents. I saw the pride in their faces every time they came to one of your games at school. I saw your dad, the very same one you argued with in town, telling people how his boy got into Notre Dame not because of a football scholarship but because of his mind. How the hell can you think he'd love you any less because of an argument?"

"You don't understand," Beau said miserably. "The day they died, that morning, I called from Notre Dame and said I wasn't coming home for Christmas. My mom was so disappointed that I heard the tears in her voice. But hey, there were always other holidays? I'd been invited to some swanky thing in Boston. My dad tore me a new one, told me I hurt my mom and that it was a family tradition to be together for the holidays. I accused him to trying to keep me a country hick. Why the hell did I get sent away

At Last

to college if I was going to be dragged back to this one horse town? I was a cold-hearted bastard."

Even though he said he didn't want to Beau was telling her everything. It was as if the story was buried inside him and the walls finally crumbled and he had to let it free. Natasha said nothing. She let him pace the room and get it all out. Maybe he'd let himself grieve and forgive himself for something that wasn't his fault.

"How could I say that to the man who gave up everything to give me and my brother everything?" Beau raged at himself. "Jesus, the man worked his fingers to the bone to build this ranch, and I pissed on it. He hung up without another word, and in my gut I knew I should've called back. But hell I was young, dumb, and full of come so I swaggered off. That night I slept so badly I got up and said fuck it I'm going home."

"I got here early Christmas morning, and they were in town at morning service in church. I was going to surprise them and apologize. I even checked my answering machine back in my dorm and heard my mom's message saying she loved me. She said 'Merry Christmas, Beau. I'll love you to the stars and beyond.'" Beau chuckled mirthlessly. "I hated that she still said it, but to her, Cody and I would always be her baby boys. Cody slapped me on the back and told me that we'd all have a laugh over it later. But that didn't happen."

Natasha got up and stopped him from pacing. Their

breakfast was forgotten, cold as she made him sit on the couch. He rested his hands on his knees and hung his head.

"It wasn't their truck that came up the driveway but the Sheriff." He heaved a long sigh. "They hit a slick spot and went into the lake and were gone. The doc said they probably froze and were unconscious before they had a chance to drown. My mom was still seatbelted in, but my dad wasn't. He could have gotten out, but there was no way he would've left Mom. So he stayed in the car with her, died with her."

"Oh, Beau," she said softly. Natasha never knew the details, only that they died in the crash, but Beau would have asked to hear it all no matter how bad. He carried it and so much guilt inside him for all these years.

"They died with my hateful words in their ears."

"Beau, look at me." Natasha grabbed his face and forced him to look at her. "They died loving you. Your mom left you a Christmas message on your answering machine. Your dad would've hugged the hell out of you, and you would have gone riding in the evening. Later on you'd all be in town with friends and laughing. Life didn't work out that way. They were taken from you. But, Beau, it wasn't your fault. Dear God, can't you see none of it was your fault? Icy roads, a slick patch, these roads are treacherous sometimes in the winter." She grabbed the book and put it on his lap. "Don't lock them away. Don't

At Last

dishonor them like that. Keep all these for your children, so they will know what wonderful people their grandparents were."

"My children, are you planning on having children with me?" His big hand cupped her cheek and caressed her skin. Natasha closed her eyes and leaned into his warm caress.

"Maybe if you weren't such a big jerk face," she murmured. "Yelling at me for doing something nice."

"I'm sorry. It was a shock, and it made me confront things I didn't want to think about. The holidays are hard, and with you here I figured I could write over the past and pretend it's all ok. But it wasn't. They're still dead."

"And you're alive. They would've wanted you to live and be happy and make babies with me," Natasha said gently.

Beau chuckled. "Yes, they would. You never know. With all the loving we've been doing, there might be a little Everett on the way."

"Maybe two," Natasha teased and watched his face turn chalk white. "Remember twins run in the family."

"Ok, then I'd better do this before we start a family." Beau reached into his pocket and pulled out a box. "Natasha Quinlan, I've loved and wanted you for so long that I can't even remember not thinking about you. Marry me and help me build a good life here, raise children here, and carry on something wonderful my parents started." He took out an elegant ring, silver with startling blue gems running along the ornate plaited lines. "Mom gave me this when I was seventeen. It was my grandmother's, and she said and I quote. . . 'For when you finally catch Natasha Quinlan.'"

She laughed. "Your mother actually said that?"

He nodded. "Remind me to tell you about the time I boldly asked your father to take you on a date and his response. Anyway, I think Mom always knew we'd be together, so now I've caught the Quinlan girl of my dreams. All she has to do is say, 'Yes, Beau, I'll marry you.' Then a new chapter of our lives begins, together."

"Well let's see. I have to think about it."

He raised an eyebrow at her. "Really?"

"No, not really." Natasha smiled wide, and her heart beat with the excitement that her dreams were coming true. "Beau Everett, it's about time you asked me to be your wife, so it's yes, always yes, and forever yes."

He pulled her across his lap and kissed her until she forgot where he ended and she began. Beau lifted his head and said gently, "Merry Christmas, Natasha soon to be Everett."

"Merry Christmas," she whispered.

"Our breakfast is cold," he murmured.

"We'll eat cereal. We've got a big dinner planned for later anyway."

"When do we start cooking?" he asked.

At Last

"Oh we've got a few hours yet. Why, what do you have planned?" she asked huskily.

"I can think of a few things." Beau gave her a devilish look before he picked her up and walked toward the stairs. Her laughter was cut off by his kiss because that Everett boy knew exactly how to celebrate Christmas right.

The End

About the Authors

Tressie Lockwood has always loved books, and she enjoys writing about heroines who are overcoming the trials of life. She writes straight from her heart, reaching out to those who find it hard to be completely themselves no matter what anyone else thinks. She hopes her readers enjoy her short stories. Visit Tressie on the web at www.tressielockwood.com.

Dahlia Rose is the best-selling author of contemporary and paranormal romance with a hint of Caribbean spice. She was born and raised on a Caribbean island and now currently lives in Charlotte, North Carolina, with her five kids, who she affectionately nicknamed "The Children of the Corn," and her biggest supporter and longtime love. She has a love of erotica, dark fantasy, sci-fi, and the things that go bump in the night. Books and writing are her biggest passions, and she hopes to open your imagination to the unknown between the pages of her books.

Ron Bracz

Made in the USA
Lexington, KY
13 February 2013